Mama's Girl

Mama's Girl

Daybreak Jones

www.urbanbooks.net

Urban Books, LLC
300 Farmingdale Road, NY-Route 109
Farmingdale, NY 11735

Mama's Girl Copyright © 2017 Daybreak Jones

ISBN 13: 978-1-62286-547-5
ISBN 10: 1-62286-547-2

First Mass Market Printing November 2017
Printed in the United States of America

10 9 8 7 6 5 4 3 2 1

This is a work of fiction. Any references or similarities to actual events, real people, living or dead, or to real locales are intended to give the novel a sense of reality. Any similarity in other names, characters, places, and incidents is entirely coincidental.

Distributed by Kensington Publishing Corp.
Submit orders to:
Customer Service
400 Hahn Road
Westminster, MD 21157-4627
Phone: 1-800-733-3000
Fax: 1-800-659-243

Mama's Girl

by

Daybreak Jones

Prologue

My eyes are open, but the darkness makes them feel closed. I know they're open because I am blinking, and I'm not asleep. I try to lift my hands to my face, but my arms are restricted. I can't move them up or to the side. I can touch my thighs. My jeans are wet and torn. When I raise my hands, I feel this cold, slick material on the back of my hand. I am sort of wrapped in something. I can't lift my legs any higher than my hands. I feel around with my hands and feet. I am inside of something. My hands and feet meet resistance.

"Hey!" I scream.

"What the hell?" is what I hear in response to my scream, and whoever said it is real close.

I start frantically moving my arms and legs as much as I can. I feel and hear my feet banging on something. I bang them harder. "Hey, somebody get me out of here!"

Suddenly a heavy hand is on my chest, holding me still. I hear a loud zip, and the light attacks my eyes. I force them closed, but I blink them open quickly.

"No! You are DOA!" he screams at me and jumps away with his hands holding his head.

"What?" I blink my eyes to seeing. "Oh, my God." I am on a metal hospital table in a body bag.

The man runs from me to a phone on a pole. "I need a physician in the morgue, stat!"

I try to get off the table. But when I look down, I see my cut-up bloody jeans and blouse.

"Jesus, help me."

I can't stand because my feet are still in the bottom of the body bag. My shoulder hurts so much that I grab it. I feel a warm liquid. Turning my head, I see blood seeping through my fingers.

"Don't move!" the man yells at me, but I try to stand anyway pulling my feet from the bag. When I swing them to the floor, blood gushes from my leg. I pull my hand from my shoulder to my thigh trying to stop the squirting. Blood keeps coming through my fingers. The room flips and spins, and I fall to the floor.

There is a doctor, maybe two, working on me. They have put an oxygen mask on me and stuck a couple IVs in my arms.

I have been shot in the shoulder, and I remember who did it.

My side and shoulder hurt. The oxygen smells like rubber. The body bag I was wrapped in is on the floor. I am hoping they will take me off this cold metal table.

"We have to move her to surgery one. I can't stop the bleeding."

I try to raise my head to see the bleeding, but a nurse holds me still.

"Relax, May. You can't move around, baby. You'll make it worse, understand?"

She sounds a lot like my mama. I nod my head. *How does she know my name?* Nobody asked me my name.

"Have the anesthesiologist in surgery one," one of the doctors says.

I look over at the guy who unzipped the body bag. He's standing by the phone pole with his eyes bucked wide open. He has a black water hose in his hand, and he is wearing a bloody white apron. I guess he is the cleanup guy. I feel like I am going to throw up, and I do.

The nurse removes my mask and turns my head to the side, and I puke all over her blue uniform pants, the metal table, and down to the body bag. I am in too much pain to really care what I vomit on. My shoulder feels like it's burning.

"My shoulder is hot," I tell them.

"We've got to move her now," the boss doctor says.

I throw up again, and they start rolling me out of the morgue. I am peeing on myself as they push me into the elevator, and I don't care. My side feels like something is trying to come out of me. There is pressure pushing from inside of me. I vomit again. The nurse wipes my lips and around my mouth. I want to tell her not to bother because I feel more coming.

"Don't worry, baby. You will be asleep soon, and the pain will stop," she says.

I doubt it. No way am I going to sleep hurting like this.

"Your thighs have been severely cut, and one of the wounds damaged an artery. When you regained consciousness and moved your legs that allowed the blood to flow. We have to stop the bleeding."

"Cuts?"

"Yes, baby, several."

"Who cut me?"

They don't have to worry about me bleeding to death because I am going to freeze to death. I am shivering to the bone, and my teeth are chattering. No way am I going to sleep now.

They have pushed me into a room with brighter lights and more people.

The nurse who sounds like my mama is still with me. She and another nurse are peeling off my clothes and sponge-bathing me. The warm water feels real good. There is a guy with a monitor behind me. He places another mask over my nose and mouth.

He asks me, "Spell your last name?"

I say, "J-o-y . . ."

I must be dreaming because Grandma and Papa are sitting on the front porch with me, and it's summer. We are watching Edith coming toward us, but it is little girl Edith not grown Edith, and she has a big bag of sunflower seeds and two sour pickles in the bags. I run down the steps toward her but, when I get to her, I am suddenly in the nightclub where I got shot. Little girl Edith is at the club with me. Dude hasn't started to shoot yet. I reach for little girl Edith, but I hear the shot and feel myself getting hit in the shoulder. I reach again for little girl Edith, but she jumps away from me and starts screaming. I am on floor in front of the bar bleeding and calling for my mama.

I wake up.

I still have on an oxygen mask, but I am no longer in that big, bright room. It's a small room with one other bed. The television is on. In its light, I see a cast and brace on my shoulder and arm. My legs are covered with the sheets, and I am too tired to try to move the sheets. I see the door opening, and a nurse walks in. I want to say something, but I can't.

It's another dream. It has to be, because I am not shot or cut, but I am at the bar where I got shot. This is my first time in a bar or club or tavern, and I am not enjoying myself at all. The place stinks of cigarettes, body sweat, beer, liquor, and cheap lady's perfume and men's cologne. In the mirror, I see myself sitting on the barstool looking at Samuel.

I'm telling him, "They are going to put my mama in jail."

"No. They will understand it was an accident."

"I don't know."

"I know. Relax. Let's get back to the hospital." He places his little glass on the bar top.

I see her in the mirror walking up behind us before she speaks: "And where are you taking this child?"

I have seen her in his car and in pictures on his phone and in his wallet. This is Samuel's wife standing behind us.

"I asked you a question, Sam. What are you doing here with this child?"

When I look at Samuel's reflection in the mirror, I am confused. His face is smiling, and he looks happy.

"Hey, baby!" he says standing and turning around. He pulls her into an embrace. "I didn't think my text went through. So you are good with going out to eat tonight?"

"What text? I saw your Porsche outside and couldn't figure out why you would be in a dive like this."

Still hugging her, he says, "Oh, me and May stopped to go over her lines. She is an understudy in the Langston play, and she's trying out for a role at Loyola. I was going to drop her off then meet you at Geno's for steaks. That is, if you're up for it."

He is still hugging her.

"Of course, baby, I would love to stop for steaks." She kisses him, breaks the embrace, and turns to me and says, "It's nice meeting you, May. I hope you get the part." She extends her hand for me to shake.

I don't know what to say, but I smile my biggest smile and shake her hand.

Suddenly, little girl Edith appears on the bar and says, "She's fucking you husband. Shoot her!"

I force myself awake.

My mouth and throat are so dry. The nurse was nice enough to put everything on my right side. He shot me in my left shoulder and moving that arm is not an option, not with the cast and the brace.

I saw him shoot me. The gun was pointed right at me. I saw the fire come out of it. Maybe he was trying to shoot her, but he shot me.

Chapter One

Six Months Earlier . . .

Cold weather is why I have to go to an alternative school. After being tardy forty-two days my junior year, the school administration kicked me out of Calumet High School. Cold, frosty mornings and I just don't get along. Standing on a corner first thing in the morning and waiting for the bus in the freezing wind is just not my thing. I didn't do it my first three years of high school, and I'm certainly not going to do it my senior year.

In my freshman, sophomore, and junior years, Uncle Doug, one of Mama's boyfriends, took me to school. He worked at the grocery store down the street from the school, so dropping me off wasn't a problem. But then his drunk butt got fired, and that left me with the bus. My mama has a car, but she won't get up to take me anywhere in the mornings. She tells me to make it the best way I can.

Mama said she caught the bus to high school so why shouldn't I. She caught the bus, all right, for one year, and then she got pregnant with me and never went back, not even to get her GED.

My best friend, Carlos, his mama wakes him up in the mornings, fixes him breakfast, and helps him get out the door. The alarm on my smart phone wakes me up, and most times when I come home from school, my mama is getting up from one of her naps. And it's not like she is tired from working. My mama doesn't have a job. She gets a check once a month, bootlegs, and gets help from her boyfriends, who she calls my uncles. I have a couple of uncles, but I never met any of the aunties who go with them.

We live in the house Grandma and Papa left Mama and me. They died five years ago, six months apart from each other, Papa first then Grandma. I miss them both every day. Our house was happier when they were alive. We were a real family with a mama and a daddy. My mama and I were more like sisters. Papa and Grandma were the grownups. After Papa and Grandma died, Mama had to be the grownup, and being an adult is hard for her.

Mama likes to have parties, and she has them all the time, but they are not happy parties. They are not birthday parties or anniversary parties like Papa and Grandma used to have. They invited real uncles and cousins and aunties over. When Grandma cooked, people would bring more than brown paper bags with bottles in them to our house. For Grandma and Papa's parties, people brought pies, cakes, bread pudding, and all kinds of stuff here. Those were happy parties.

Mama's parties are "just because" parties: just because somebody's check came, just because somebody hit the number, just because somebody got divorced, or just because it's Friday night. "Just because" parties are not real parties.

Mama and her friends love to party and act happy, but their eyes are sad even when their faces are grinning. It's a weird thing to see, a smiling face with sad eyes, but I see it all the time at Mama's parties. Papa told me a person's eyes tell their story. If that's true, and I believe it is, then Mama and her loud partying friends are sad, despite the laughs that come out of their mouths.

Well, because Mama spends her time with her partying friends and her boyfriends, I have to get myself up and out in the mornings. A person would think that a mother would take her only child to school but, nope, that's not the case with Gloria Joyce. She brags about me making the A-B honor roll, but she won't take me to school.

My mama told me getting up in the mornings would add stress to her life, and stress would give her wrinkles, and wrinkles would make her look older, which cannot happen by any means because she has to stay looking young for the uncles, which I don't understand, because all the uncles look old. My mama looks too good and too young to be bothered with any of her boyfriends.

My mama is fine, beautiful really. She could be a supermodel—well, a short one. I have seen models who aren't tall. She could be one. People say I look like her, but Mama is way prettier than me. We share the same light complexion, but Mama's lips are narrow where mine are thick. Men say they like my thick lips, and I like my lips, but Mama's thin ones seem to balance her face. Her nose is pointed, and mine is wide and kind of round. She says she wishes she had my nose but, again, hers matches her face. What makes her so pretty is that every part on her face is balanced. No part overshadows another. People are always mistaking us for sisters, and she doesn't bother to correct them.

Once, the truant officer from my old high school came by the house. He wouldn't talk to Mama or come into the house because he thought she was my sister, and that we were trying to run a game on him. After she showed him her driver's license, he gave her my attendance record still standing on the porch. He told her I would be transferred to the alternative school because of my tardiness. In his very next breath, he commented on her not having on a wedding ring and asked her out to dinner. My mama smiled and questioned him on his ability to stop the transfer. He had no power in that area, he told her. Still smiling, she closed the door in his face.

The alternative school isn't that bad. It doesn't start until ten o'clock, and there is a bus that picks students up. And by going to the alternative school, I will be graduating this year. If I had stayed at Calumet, I wouldn't graduate until next year because I failed my eight a.m. English class last year due to my tardiness. That got me really mad because I got mostly A's on my assignments despite being late. School policy is statewide, the principal told my mama. There was nothing he could do.

At the alternative school, I can retake English at an accelerated rate so I will graduate this year, which should make me happy but, honestly, I just want to stop going to school. Being finished with it will be a relief. I want high school to be over.

We live on Eighty-ninth and Morgan, and the alternative school is all the way out on 115th Street, and it's a locked campus, and all the extracurricular activities revolve around school stuff. I joined the computer club, but only because of the late bus driver. He's an actor and model, and he drives the bus part time, and he is too fine, and the way he looked at me from the start told me he was interested.

His father owns the bus company, and my mama says his family has money. I have seen their buses all my life and never thought that it was a family name on the side of them: Talbert Transportation Service. His name is Samuel Talbert. He has curly hair, prefect white teeth, smooth bright skin, green eyes, and he's tall. He showed me some pictures of himself in magazine ads. And since he models and acts, the whole world must think he is fine, not just Mama and me.

Another good thing about the alternative school, besides Samuel, is Carlos going there too. He got kicked out of Calumet for making and selling fake state IDs. They kicked him out even with him being the starting forward and the highest scorer on the team. He could have gone to jail and gotten kicked out of the school system for good making those phony IDs, but his mama begged the school administration not to report him to the police. Mama says she did more than beg Mr. Anderson, the principal, but Mama never has anything nice to say about Ms. Carol.

They grew up next door to each other just like Carlos and me, and they were best friends too. Now, they give each other phony smiles and halfhearted waves when they pass. Whatever happened between them happened years ago, and only they know what it was. Not even Grandma or Papa knew what stopped them from being best friends.

Carlos and I were best friends before we knew the difference between boy and girl, and we are still best friends today, despite knowing. None of his girlfriends can stand me, and I don't care. Our friendship is stronger than any boyfriend-girlfriend relationship. We listen to each other, and I tell him when a girl is a tramp. Sometimes a pretty face fools him. Like a lot of dark-skinned boys, he attracts girls with light complexions. I guess opposites do attract, and since he's tall and plays basketball, the girls really sweat him. But I keep the tramps away, and he does the same for me, but he's not sure about Samuel yet.

Samuel is five years older than us, so Carlos can't get any real info on him, but he told me to take my time with him and not to have sex with him. He said older dudes always want to sex up a high school girl and then move on to another one. That much he is certain of. I hope Samuel does want to sex me up because I sure want him to sex me up. If I waited on Carlos to decide who I should have sex with, I would still be a virgin. As far as he is concerned no guy is good enough for me to do it with.

I like that about him though.

What I don't like about him is that he always keeps me waiting. I waved on the bus this morning because he said his mama was letting him drive her new car to school. I see the new car out there warming up, but no Carlos. My stomach is growling and bubbling a little bit from the three chocolate éclairs I ate last night. I knew I was overdoing it when I ate the second one, but they were so fresh and tasted so good. I hold my stomach while looking out of the door window for Carlos.

His mama bought a Cadillac two weeks ago, and this is the first time she's letting him drive it to school. I'm hyped about riding in it myself.

The pearl white exterior is too fly. *Maybe I can run to the bathroom before he comes out.* Nope. I see his slow butt coming down the steps now. He stops at the bottom of the step because Mooky has run up on him probably begging for money. Mooky will beg a hungry baby for a sip off a bottle. He wasn't always like that. At one time we all looked up to him, but not now. Carlos hands him a dollar and Mooky jogs off. I could go out and meet him at the car, but I'm going to make him walk over here and ring the doorbell. My mama should really enjoy hearing the chimes this morning.

Man! Carlos is clean. He is wearing a new off-white leather bomber jacket and a matching cap. Kid is trying to match his mama's new car. *Since he wants to roll like that, let me slip into my mama's white fox jacket.*

I open the front door for him, and the cold air comes in with him. I open the door wide. The frigid blast and the chimes should disturb Mama's comfort.

"Wow! Baby girl, you are looking mighty good this Friday morning. Good enough to be riding in a Cadillac." He grins.

Even in the low tone he is speaking in now, his big, dog-barking voice commands my attention. When he talks, his voice always fills up the inside of my head.

I take a step back from the door and tell him, "Man, I look good enough to be riding in a Cadillac every morning. These things I thought you knew." I hit him with a smile from my newly dentist-whitened teeth.

"Yeah, well, whatever. But you do look good this morning. Does Gloria know you wearing her fox?"

I suck my pearly whites and answer, "This is my coat. You want to see the inscription?"

"Yeah." His grin challenges me to show the label.

"I'll show you later. Let's ride."

"Yeah, we better get on out of here before Gloria wakes up and peels her fur coat off your back."

He's right about that. My mama doesn't play about her furs, so I push him a little to get him moving out the door. After feeling how cold it is out here, I want to keep the fox on.

Once we get in the Cadillac, I am very impressed. It's a real nice car with soft beige leather seats and a thick carpet, and it has that new-car smell, which is being bullied by Carlos's cologne.

"You like the car, don't you? Yeah, I know you do." He is cheesing big time as he pulls away from the curb, leaning on the armrest. Profiling is what he calls this leaning while driving.

"So, who are you getting with after school? I know you didn't beg Ms. Carol for the car just to drive me to school."

He flips his four fingers up like a seal. He thinks that is a cool gesture, and he says, "I didn't have to beg her. I told her I needed the car and I picked up the keys," he says, still leaning hard almost touching the driver's window.

"Yeah, okay. You can tell that to somebody who don't know. I am certain that you were on your knees for at least an hour, begging. So, stop frontin,' and tell me: who is it?"

"You know Michelle Pickens?"

"Yeah, I know Michelle. A brown girl with a big butt and wigs. She's in my computer lab."

"She wears wigs?" he asks sitting up straight behind the steering wheel.

"Boy, please, everybody at school knows her hair comes from the Korean shop on Ashland. I hope you ain't serious about her. Ms. Carol will hurt her feelings too bad if you bring her home. Michelle is smart and all, but you know how your mama is about fake hair."

"How do you know she wears wigs?"

It is official. I have the bubble guts and need to use the bathroom, like right now. "You can't see her scalp, stupid, and her hair is different lengths and different styles every day. You had to have noticed. But, then, maybe you didn't. Boys can act so dumb when they trying to get some pussy."

I pull down the visor on the passenger side looking for a mirror. The Cadillac has a lighted one. I pull out my eyeliner to add a little flair to my look and to distract myself from thinking about the bathroom.

"I ain't trying to get some. I now already got some it." He leans back on the armrest. "And I am not a boy," he huffs.

"You have been doing it to Michelle?" With the eyeliner in my hand, I notice that my eyes are perfectly lined. There is nothing I can do to make them better. I flip the visor up and drop the eyeliner back in my purse. "I thought she was smart," I say in response to his not answering my question.

"What?" he asks with his narrow face twisted. "She is smart. Her doing it with me doesn't stop her from being smart."

I turn to face him because he has obviously forgotten who he's talking to. "You don't love her. And I know this because you haven't said a word about her to me. What, is she going to Ohio State with you next year? Does she even know about the basketball scholarship? The answers are no and no. If you loved her, you would have told your secret without fear of her trying to play you. And since you sexed her up without being in love with her, she's not that smart."

I have never been in love, but I do enjoy sex. I figured out that it's not important for me to be in love, but the boys have to be head over heels in love with me before they get close to having sex with me. I have a shoebox full of love letters and greeting cards all confessing undying love. Not to mention the constant supply of Nikes, Adidas, and Reeboks gym shoes from Walter. When guys are in love, they try harder to please. In my opinion, any girl who gives it up to a dude who is not in love with her isn't smart.

Carlos blows an exasperated breath. "You don't know everything, May."

"About you I do."

"You make me sick thinking that."

"Whatever, but you know it's true."

I do know him well, and what he's going to do next is reach into his pants pocket and pull out a roll of tropical fruit Lifesavers and suck on one all the way to school and not say another word unless I do.

We are about six blocks from school. I can make it without asking Carlos to make a bathroom stop.

When he pops the candy in his mouth I say, "So where are you taking her?"

He smacks on the Lifesaver deciding if he will answer.

"Oh, well, thanks for the ride to school anyway."

He huffs again, and then he says, "My mama had four tickets to a play about Langston Hughes, and she gave them to me."

He's talking to me, but he's not looking at me. His eyes are straight ahead, which is cool because he is driving, but I know his not looking at me is part of the attitude he's trying to give me. I really couldn't care less about him being upset. What has my interest now is the tickets. Samuel, my bus driver boyfriend, is in the Langston Hughes play.

"Four tickets? Who else is going with you?"

"Nobody. I was going to try to sell the other two at the door. It's a matinee right after school."

"I know all about the play," I say grabbing his shoulder and shaking it. That's a mistake because the car swerves a little. "Oops, sorry, but Samuel is in that play. He hasn't driven the bus all week because of the matinee schedule. I'm going with you guys."

"Huh?"

"You heard me. I'm going. And I'll sell the other ticket for you so your girlfriend won't have to see you hustling tickets on a date. Trust me, it's not something a girl wants to see."

His whole face gets into a frown. "You ain't doing it for me. You're doing it to go see that Samuel dude. Mr. Peters from across the alley drives for the same bus company, and he says dude is a spoiled punk, a rich boy crybaby."

Now he is looking at me.

"You're tripping," I say looking away, and he is. I know envy when I hear it. Samuel has money, and for a grown man like Mr. Peters to be talking about him, it must be quite a bit.

"And I heard he be dogging girls because he has a little loot. He took two girls to his prom, and they didn't know they were going to be part of a three-people date. Each one thought they were going alone with him."

"Be serious."

"I am. Edith told me about it. He's a dog."

"Edith?" *Why would she tell him and not me? That's girlfriend talk. I am going to have to check in with her. She's holding on to vital information.* "How could he do that? The girls at the school had to be talking about who they were going to prom with."

"They didn't go to his school, and they were both sophomores. He played them to make himself look like a player. He's twenty-two, and, if you're not careful, he's going to play you too. Hold up." He pauses. "You talking about my mama tripping over Michelle's wigs. What do you think Gloria gonna say when she sees dude?"

"She's met Samuel, twice. He came over Sunday and brought Peking duck." Which actually is the only time we have had anything like a date. The other time my mama met him was when she came up on the bus to see him after I told her he gave me his cell phone number. The bus was dropping me off, and she pushed her way past me onto the bus.

She wasn't loud or anything and spoke in a tone only he could hear: "So, my daughter tells me you and her are talking on the phone. I don't have a problem with that as long as things stay on the phone. If anything else happens like movies, dinner, concerts, or any kind of date with her you need to ask me in advance. You're grown and she's not. Let's not complicate things. For now, the only place you can visit her is at our home. And if I find out that this bus has veered off its regular route, you will wish to God that you never met her or me."

I thought for sure Samuel was out of my life after that, but he wasn't. We had dinner at the house Sunday, and we talk on the phone every night, and he said he was going to figure out a way he could take me to my senior prom. I'm not sure I want him to take me to prom, but we will see.

"Wait, last Sunday? Tell me that wasn't his red Porsche on the block."

"He has a little red car. I don't know what kind it is. Why, is a Porsche fly?"

"Very fly. Did he bring his wife and kids to Sunday dinner?"

"Only a wife. He doesn't have children."

"So, his wife was over your mama's house?"

"No, just him and the Peking duck."

"You telling me Gloria knows dude is married, and she let him come to dinner?" He quickly tries to look from traffic to my eyes. He thinks he can tell if I am lying by my eyes. He can't. I lie to him all the time.

"What you are forgetting, Carlos, is that we are talking about my mama, not yours. When my mama found out his family owns Talbert Transportation Service, Samuel was in. That's it, and that's all."

"That ain't right."

It may not be right, but that's my mama. Had Samuel been ugly, twenty-two, and poor, his age would have been a problem, but at six feet three inches, fine, and wealthy, Samuel is okay with Mama. Matter of fact, when he came over Sunday, she was a little too okay with him as far as I am concerned.

She started asking him about his daddy and any older brothers. It was embarrassing. After dinner, though, he had to leave. She wouldn't go for us catching a movie on Sunday evening. I think things are going to go pretty smooth with Samuel at home as long as I go at Mama's pace. She can't be rushed about him if I want to keep seeing him. And I made up my mind Sunday that I want to keep seeing him.

I like how it feels to be in his company. He makes me feel more mature, more grown up. I try not to say silly things around him. When we are on the school bus, I talk about adult topics like the news and stuff. But Sunday, I was at home and so relaxed that we ended up talking about things I really have an interest in: movies, actors, concerts that are coming to town, outlet malls, and acting. We were sitting on the couch in the front room, and he said he enjoyed being around me at my home because I was more myself.

Mama had said we could sit up front a little before he left, so we were sitting on the couch talking. We kissed once, and while we were kissing, I saw his ding-a-ling rising in his pants. Now, that was not much different from the high school boys I date. Kissing gets them started too. Being honest, though, he kissed me so good that I got kind of started too.

I am not the least bit shy about what pleases me and, when I saw him rising in his jeans, I dropped my hand in his lap. It was a long, slow kiss, so I got a good estimate of his size. It took me twelve slow-counted seconds to drag my finger the length of his ding-a-ling. He's not only the oldest boy I've dated but the biggest, too, and I am a little concerned about that.

Mama must have been watching from the dining room because as soon as the kiss stopped, she appeared in the living room announcing that it was time for my company to leave.

She had to have startled Samuel, because he jumped right up, and my mama's eyes went straight to his bulge. Then she looked at me and left. Over her shoulder, she told me again it was time for Samuel to leave. Mama is a trip.

The problem now though is how to get her to let me go to the matinee with Carlos and Michelle. I told her last week that Samuel was in the play, so she knows he will be there. I could say it's a computer club field trip. No, that won't work. I got to think of something.

Our school doesn't have a student parking lot, so Carlos pulls up to the front door to let me out because he will have to drive down the block to look for a parking spot, and he knows I am not walking in this cold weather.

Getting out of the car I say, "See you at two forty-five. And don't try to act like you forgot. If you go without me, I'll tell Michelle about you-know-what." And he knows what the you-know-what is. He always knows.

"May, you need to stop with that 'pee in the bed' threat. It doesn't work anymore. Damn, girl, I was nine years old when that happened."

"No, you were thirteen. And leave without me, and we will see if it works."

I try to slam the door for emphasis, but the Cadillac door won't slam. It pulls closed on its own power. Carlos laughs at my attempt and drives off.

I make it to computer lab early, so I run into the bathroom to relieve my stomach. I don't usually go number two in public, but the chocolate éclair has moved through me, changing my normal actions. Besides, there are only two girls in computer lab, and Michelle is usually late, so I should have some privacy.

Michelle and I are not really friends, but since we will be spending time together after school today, I really don't want to stink bomb her. On the first day of class, I attempted a friendly conversation, but the forced smile she responded with crushed that idea.

As soon as I sit on the toilet, I start relieving myself and hear the door opening. I reach into my purse feeling for cologne or breath spray. Nothing. Oh, well.

I hear Michelle coughing in response to the odor. I want to laugh out loud but don't.

"Is there a boy in here? This is the ladies' room. That is so rude of you to come in here and do that. I am reporting you to Mr. Griffin."

"It's me, Michelle, May."

"Oh, I am sorry. I thought it was a boy fouling the air."

She didn't think I was a boy. She has to see my shoes and purse on the floor. There is only one stall in the small bathroom. Girls like Michelle annoy me, acting like their poop doesn't stink.

I go on and finish what I came in here to do. Unfortunately, chocolate makes me gassy, so gaseous noise accompanies the bodily function.

"Oh, my God, really, May?"

I can no longer hold the laugh. Laughing, I tell her, "Leave. It is only going to get worse."

I hear her heels tapping on the tile and the door squeaking open.

Being in this situation makes me think about Edith. She is my only real female friend remaining from Calumet. When we were little kids, Edith would fart in public, and no one ever suspected her because she looked so cute and innocent. We had a lot of good laughs behind her farts. I need to call her and ask her about Samuel. We haven't spoken in a couple of weeks. Me being forced to the alternative school has put an unexpected distance between us. Well, my school transfer and her joining church, but I miss my girl.

Chapter Two

Carlos doesn't leave me after school. He is parked at the curb waiting for me. I knew he wouldn't and not because of the "pee in the bed" threat. He didn't leave me because he now knows that Michelle wears wigs. My best friend in the world is trying to figure out a way to dump the girl sitting next to him in his mama's new Cadillac. I open the back door and get in.

It's not really his fault that he wants to break up with her. He can't help it. He is like his mama. Ms. Carol has a hang-up about long hair, and she has passed it on to him. His mama's hair hangs down to the top of her butt, and Carlos's braids hang past his shoulders. The only way Michelle can stay the apple of his eye is if her wig topples off and reveals a head full of long hair.

It's really sad because he liked her, but now he doesn't have a clue why he doesn't like her. I will bet twenty dollars to a nickel that he is relieved that I am sitting in this car with them.

"Oh, my God, how much Prada do you have on? I am almost choking back here."

Carlos has gym his last hour. He must have showered in the cologne. I have to open the window halfway because the sweet fumes have my eyes watering.

"It ain't all that strong as you putting on." He sniffs the air and himself.

Mama is the one who insisted on getting him cologne for Christmas: "A fragrance is a good gift for a young man. It makes him conscious of his hygiene." I don't know which would be worse: his gym class funk or the overdone fragrance. Next year, he will be getting clothing from the Joyce family.

I decided to tell my mama the truth about the play since I couldn't think up a believable lie. She surprised me and said I could go, but I have to find out exactly what time the play ends so she can pick me up afterward. Mama is not giving Samuel and me any time alone. She has never been this strict with boys before, but Samuel is not really a boy. He is a man, a very good-looking man.

Michelle's curly wig really doesn't look that bad. I would wear it if I wore wigs, but my hair, although thin, hangs halfway down my back.

I shouldn't have told Carlos about Michelle's wigs. The boy should have been left ignorant and happy.

How did he have sex with her and not know she was wearing a wig? One of the first things guys do is play with my hair while we're doing it. I guess Carlos doesn't run his fingers through the girl's hair when he gets sexually riled up.

Obviously, he didn't run his fingers through Michelle's, or maybe he did and her wigs were secured. Who knows and who cares? That's between him and his wig-wearing girlfriend. I want to roll the car window up from the cold, but I still smell his cologne. Good thing I have on my mama's fox.

To get a conversation started I ask, "Michelle, do you go to a lot of plays?"

I see she has rolled her window down too. If his Prada fumes are strong back here, she must be getting gassed. Poor baby, she got hit by my stink bomb first thing in the morning and now Carlos's overdone cologne.

"Yes, I do. Most of my family are thespians. My father has been in theater for over thirty years. He is an active member of the Chicago Actors Guild. And he is costarring in this play along with two of my cousins. They all have leading roles. The family is so proud. I was going to wait until we got seated to spring it all on you, Carlos, but I can't hold it in any longer. When you told me you had tickets to this performance, I could have burst with joy.

"I have actually performed at the theater in over five productions. It's by far my favorite venue. My father and my cousins love it as well. We are in for a dynamic threat. Matinee or not, believe me, they will be putting their best foot forward. So, the short answer to your question is yes, I go to the theater often. And what about you, May?"

Oh, my God. I thought she only talked that way in front of teachers. Who is in the front seat, a girl from the South Side of Chicago or some proper prissy prep from the North Shore? Since I'm certain she is from the South Side, the wig-wearer must be pretending to be something she is not, and one good act deserves another.

So, I say, "Girl, I like da movies, but I'll try anythang once," with as much bass as possible in my voice. If she wants to play prissy girl, I'll play thug girl.

"The movies is better dan TV, but wid da TV I can play my video games. I wish I could hook up my video games at the show, smoke some weed, and play *Saint's Row* on a big-ass movie screen. Dat would be dope." I slam my fist into the back of her seat for emphasis. "But wid dem plays at the theater, all ya do is sit and watch people act out stuff, right? I ain't sho' I'ma like it."

She answers with, "Actually, there is a little more to it than that, May." Her left hand is in the air with fingers twinkling. "Plays are human drama, and depending on the actor's ability the drama should pull you in totally. And since the performance is live with real, breathing thespians, I think it will hold your interest more than any movie or video game."

Michelle turns to face me. She's looking as if I am a kid who ate a black jellybean and didn't like it, and she is trying to convince me to try the yellow jellybean.

"I don't know 'bout dat. Dem video games be real, especially if you smoke a blunt. I can sit all day in front of da tube and be into dem games. I be sweatin' and everythang. A play will have to be real good to be better dan dat!" I have to bite the inside of my jaw to stay in character because I want to laugh out loud.

"May, stop!" Carlos interrupts my performance. "Michelle, she is messing with you. May has been in three plays at that theater, and when we were kids, her grandma had season tickets at two theaters downtown. She would take us to plays almost every Sunday: me, May, and this girl named Edith. We all loved going to the plays. That's how we got into drama when we were kids. All three of us were in *The Lion King*."

She looks from me to Carlos and says, "*The Lion King?* You two were in that performance? I tried so hard to get into that production, and they accepted you two?"

Oh, my God, what does she mean by "you two"? As if we couldn't possibly have been good enough actors to get in *The Lion King*. *What I should do is reach over this seat and snatch that curly mess of a wig off her thespian head and see how proper she really is.* I haven't seen a black woman yet who didn't go straight hood when their hair was messed with.

"I think May's grandma knew people, but I don't know how it happened for sure. We were so young. It seems like another lifetime, don't it, May?"

Carlos is trying to make eye contact with me in the rearview mirror. I look away because he should have let me run my little skit on Miss Prissy Pants.

"Yeah, it does, and that's kind of sad. So, let's go back to talking about this play. Who are your cousins, Michelle, and what's your father's name?" I don't want to start thinking about or talking about the past or my grandma. That gets me down. And I'm not trying to be gloomy right now. I want to keep the artsy girl talking. If she says enough of the wrong things to me, snatching off her wig will be easy.

"Darnell and Dominique Knight are my cousins, and my father is Russell Pickens."

I know both of her cousins and her dad. Her cousin Dominique and I got into some heavy petting in the director's office when I was about eleven. He told me he loved me and brought me one of his mama's diamond rings. He asked for it back a week later, but I told him it was lost. It got lost all right, right in my jewelry box next to the diamond earrings Papa gave me.

"I remember your dad: a tall, thin guy with intense black eyes. He ran the drama program with the park district. Carlos, Edith, and me used to go to his class at Foster Park. I stopped going about four years ago. The best play we did was *West Side Story*."

"Yes, that's him."

I like her father, a lot. He took time with the kids and treated everyone the same. Her father gets her a pass today if she can shut up. I look out the window and notice that Carlos has gotten on the expressway and that we are driving by the paint factory.

"Hey, Carlos, do you remember the Christmas play we did in there?"

"Yep. They had commercials about it and everything."

We were about eight. The company made a commercial out of part of the play. I wonder what happened to that money. It was a major commercial and played all over the country. The pay had to be substantial. My mama spent and spends money like there is no tomorrow. My grandma used to say money burns a hole in her pocket.

Acting was cool back then, but after my grandparents died everything just went sort of bland for me. Now that I'm thinking about it, this will be the first play I have gone to since they died.

"I got started acting in the park program too," Michelle says, rolling up her window. "If it weren't for the program, I doubt that I would have gotten into drama, but because there were so many kids doing it, I got involved. It was like going to a school that was all fun. You know, we probably met back then and just don't remember it."

Michelle turns around in her seat to face me. She has a large, warm smile and bright eyes, and I can feel that she is genuinely trying to be friendly, so I give her a smile and decide that I will try to be nice too.

"I am sure we met. We had to. It will come to us later, girl," I say in my nice sister-girl voice.

"Well, y'all know we had to meet at the end-of-the-year play at city hall. That was when all the park classes got together and put on one performance, so we had to cross paths there," Carlos offers.

"Oh, darn. I have to take this thing off. If my daddy sees me in a wig, he will trip, and he might be at the performance." She pulls about five bobby pins from her head and removes the brown curly wig from her head, revealing cornrows that, once she lets down, hang well past her shoulders. Carlos takes his eyes from the road to give her natural hair a quick look. He's grinning from ear to ear. And I am honestly happy for him because now I think he will at least give the girl a chance, which is what he wants to do.

"Why do you wear a wig?" he asks.

"It's my parents. They are in business producing this natural hair growth grease, and the whole family has to use it, but the product works best when the hair is braided, so while we are in testing my hair has to stay in braids. I wear wigs for the different styles. But if my daddy saw me in a wig he would think I was damaging the study results. So, to stop all that, I sneak a wig on when I get to school. That way I can have a different style when I want one."

"Does the grease work?" I ask. Not that I need it or that my mama would let me use anything but lanolin in my hair. Three generations of women with jet-black hair—my mama, my grandma, and me—and nothing stronger than lanolin and mild heat has been in our hair, but I do want to know if her daddy's product grows hair. I roll my window up to hear her clearly.

"Yes, it's been working in our family forever. The test is for the manufacturer. We get more money if the results show so much growth over a certain period of time. They actually cut my hair at the start to measure new growth. Over fifty percent of this is new growth." She extends her braids. "And they have only been measuring a little over three months. So, it works. Which we already knew, but the people buying the formula didn't know it."

She is prissy. It's not an act with her. No matter what she's talking about she uses correct English and that snippy tone. Having never spent any time alone with her at school, I just assumed she was like all the rest of us South-siders, but she really is a prissy, proper girl.

"Daddy says the sale money will pay for college for my brothers and me, and buy us acres of land in Alabama. His plan is to build a new house on the land so, when he retires, he and Mama can move down South with no worries.

"The deal is pretty much done with the last measurement of my hair, and my aunts'. The dollar amount of the deal I'm not privy to, but I believe it's going to be enough to change the whole family's life for the better. Daddy has already sold our home on Racine, and he said we will be moving to Longwood with or without the sale of the formula. But with the sale things are going to be all the better."

Uh-oh. I don't like the icky feeling stirring about in my stomach and the back of my head. I know exactly what it is. I labeled it last year when I found out about Carlos's basketball scholarship.

"My mama says Daddy must be in a lucky cycle because of his promotion at work, his part in the play, and the company's interest in purchasing the formula. She started calling him Midas." Michelle giggles.

It's a common feeling for me. I feel it every time one of the girls from school gets picked up by a parent in a Mercedes or BMW. I feel it when I hear them talking about going shopping or getting their hair done with their mamas. I feel it when they talk about their family life, which includes both mother and father. I feel it when I see boys who swore their love to me with other girls even if I don't want them anymore, and I'm feeling it now listening to Michelle talking about her parents' financial windfall.

"I must admit I love it all. Daddy bought a new car, and weekly allowances for my brothers and me have gone from fifty dollars to two hundred. I can actually go to a mall and shop for an outfit every weekend now. And I know it's not all my daddy. My mama is a CPA, and her firm has just promoted her as well, but all eyes are on Daddy now, and I am happy for him. I can remember arguments between him and Mama about his acting not paying bills. It hasn't always been good for him."

I want all her hair to fall out, and her daddy to be kicked out of the actors guild, and her mama to contract a horrible disease that will leave her deaf, blind, and disfigured. I want her and her family broke and living in a homeless shelter. I want Carlos to get her pregnant so she will get an abortion that will cause her to bleed to death. I want her daddy's hair formula to eat through her skin and give her bone cancer.

"You two have been letting me ramble on for most of the ride. Enough about me. One of you tell me about your parents."

Okay. Let's see. My mama dates older men for money and sells liquor after hours, and Carlos's mama works at the hospital part time, gets social security, and hosts weekend crap games, and neither one of us knows a damn thing about our fathers. This is what I would say if it wouldn't hurt Carlos. Talking about our unknown fathers always upsets him, so I say nothing.

What I want to do is say something to hurt Michelle. I want to say something very cruel to her, something that will fill her big brown eyes with tears. I want to hurt her. So much so that when Carlos pulls into the theater parking lot, I bolt from the Cadillac before he can stop and park the vehicle. I know me, and I know what my mouth is capable of.

I run through the glass theater doors, pretending I have an emergency, and I go straight into the ladies' bathroom, which is to the side of the ticket window. Thank God, the small bathroom is empty. I run the cold water into the black marble face bowl and place my wrist under the flow and began to take deep breaths. I have to calm myself.

Carlos's mama taught me this technique after I made a fool of myself at a party for him. When I found out Carlos didn't lose his college basketball scholarship after he was expelled from Calumet, I got so angry that I cursed him and his mama. I didn't know why I was angry with them, but I was livid. And it was at the party they threw because of the good news. They invited only me. I was the only person they shared the news with, and I couldn't be happy with them. How I felt inside wouldn't allow it, just like how I am feeling about Michelle now will not let me treat her nice.

If I had not gotten out of that car, I would have talked about her and her daddy something awful. The icky feeling would have gotten tight inside my head, and it wouldn't have eased up until I hurt her feelings and made her cry. Once she was hurt, the icky feeling inside my head would have gone away. I don't like being this way. It's hard to make and keep friends like this. The running water is becoming icy cold, but I hold my wrist in place.

Man, this is a bright bathroom. It's really weird how a bathroom could be so well lit when it's got such a dark décor: black and gray tiled floors, and black marble tile on the walls, counters, and stall doors. The light is bright in this black and gray room.

My reflection is clear in the mirror. It must be a makeup mirror with slight magnification because my face looks a little larger than normal. I pull my wrist from the stream of cold water and think about splashing my face, but my face is made up to perfection, so rinsing it is out of the question.

Concentrating on the deep breaths will calm me. I won't have to splash my face if I breathe the right way. Cutting the water off I begin taking the cleansing breaths Ms. Carol taught me how to take after I cursed her out at Carlos's scholarship party.

We were sitting in their living room where she was holding me in her arms while I cursed her like a sailor. I called her every nasty name I could think of, and I said every hurtful thing that ran through my mind. I had lost it, and she knew it. She settled me down by getting me to breathe in deep through my nose and breathe out slow through my mouth.

I just couldn't understand how Carlos could be so lucky. How could he get expelled from school and still have his scholarship? It pissed me off because I have no substantial plans after high school, and Carlos does.

While I was in her embrace and breathing, she began to tell me about emotions and feelings, and how we must label them to deal with them. If we don't know the emotion we are feeling, it can rule us. And as women, she said, it is all the more important to label our emotions because they run strong through us. She held me in her arms and began listing and explaining emotions that I might be feeling.

When she got to envy and explained it as me wishing I had what someone else had and becoming angry with the person for having what I wanted, all of that hot, icky feeling that was inside my head eased out with a breath. Hearing out loud what I was feeling inside helped to calm me. She labeled my emotion. She told me that although I had told everyone I didn't want to go to college, I probably really did want to go and was mad with Carlos because he had a way to attend.

I cried like a baby in her arms. She sent Carlos out of the room and let me boohoo real good. I didn't want to be envious of Carlos or anyone else, but the truth is I am a very envious person, and I have to check the emotion when it first appears because it will have me tripping.

Envy is what I am feeling toward Michelle, and I cannot allow it to get the best of me. I take another deep breath.

What am I envious of?

The money her father may get.

The money her father has.

The fact that she has both a father and a mama, and they both seem to care about her.

What can I do to lessen the envious feeling?

Be grateful for my mama.

Remember the love of Papa and Grandma.

And realize that Michelle will never be as fine as me. Oh, now that makes me feel much better.

With the envy subsiding, I notice that envy isn't the only emotion stirring around inside of me. Being at a theater has me thinking of and missing my grandma. And I always try my best not to go down that sad road, but coming to the theater and thinking so much about her has me with "one foot on that road," as she would say.

And, not to mention, I am little nervous about seeing Samuel. He's not expecting me. His wife could be here for all I know. There's a lot on my mind, and I did the right thing getting into this bathroom. There is no telling what might have come out of my mouth.

"Envy, sadness, and anxiousness ran me up in here," I say out loud to my reflection in the mirror. "Understanding and confidence will get your fine self back out there. Let's go, girl. Shake it off, go on out there and smile, and then smile some more."

I take another five deep, cleansing breaths and decide to leave.

Michelle is coming into the bathroom as I am exiting.

"Are you okay?"

I see her lipstick is almost smeared off. She and Carlos must have gotten into a little lip action before she came in to check on me.

"Oh, I'm okay, girl, just a little gas from the cheeseburger at school, and I didn't want Carlos to hear me poot. He would have never let me live it down." I look at her directly, making a reference to her attitude earlier this morning in the lab bathroom.

Her round eyes widen and she nods. "Oh, I know, boys remember our poots forever. Like it makes us nasty, and they do it out loud and laugh, but let a girl part company and we are stinky heifers for eternity. It's not fair. Well, if you are okay, I'll meet you at our seats."

She enters a stall, and I walk out of the bright black and gray bathroom.

Behind the braided black velvet robes, I see Carlos towering over a crowd of boisterous little kids. He is handing the tickets to the usher and being let through the robes.

The lobby is filled with what looks like third and fourth graders. Carlos looks like Gulliver, a giant among dwarfs. The kids are loud and busy. It must be like three or four different classes. I see two teachers trying to control them as best they can. At least the kids are in a line.

Carlos passes the ticket window and gets to me. "Mama said the tickets were student passes. I assumed she meant high school student passes. I didn't know we would be here with munchkins. Where did Michelle go?"

I was right about him and Michelle. He has lipstick smeared on his neck. I ran out of his car in a frantic state, and he takes time to make out before he checks on me, bastard. I don't tell him about the smear on his neck.

"She is in the bathroom right behind us." I have to yell because the kids are so loud.

"That's pretty cool about her hair and the wigs, huh?" He is yelling too.

"Yeah. Now you don't have to dump her."

He looks like he did when I beat him at *Madden:* shocked stupid. "How did you know I was thinking about dumping her?" he asks. He doesn't yell, and he looks behind me for Michelle.

"Boy, I know you." I dismiss him with a wave of my hand.

I spot Samuel across the lobby, and he has seen me. He is making a beeline through the disruptive kids in our direction. He has on a pair of Levi's, a white sweatshirt, and a pair of all-white Reeboks. My baby looks fresh.

"Here comes your old-ass boyfriend, and here is your ticket. I'm gonna stand over there and wait for Michelle. Oops, I almost forgot, not that you care, but Walter told me to remind you that he is stopping by tonight. He said he had something real important to tell you."

"I haven't forgot Walter is coming over, and it's really crude of you to say I don't care about him. I can have more than one male friend."

He just doesn't want me to be with Samuel. He couldn't care less about me forgetting Walter's visit.

"Yeah, right. You ain't been thinking about nothing but him." He nods his head in Samuel's direction. He walks to the other side of the ticket window, and once there he shoots Samuel a hateful, teeth-baring look that only I can see. Carlos is a trip. But who cares? Samuel is grinning and happy to see me.

"Mmmm, don't you look good." He bends down to hug me. "I almost didn't recognize you in that fur jacket. I thought you were one of the teachers. Who did you come here with?"

The sound of Samuel's voice reminds me of a motorcycle cruising down the block. The way he talks, the rhythm of his words, makes me think of Grandma's humming. He stands straight up, releasing me too soon from the snug hug. I could stay linked to him for another hour. He smells good, too, sort of like caramel.

"My next-door neighbor and his girlfriend brought me, but Mama is picking me up," I shout over the kids.

"Hold up, your mama is not here?" he says into my ear.

"Not yet. She'll be here ten minutes before the play ends," I say into his ear.

"Baby, I was on standby for this performance and just found out they won't need me. My brother's apartment is right across the street. If you want, we can go over there and be alone for the duration of the play."

"Just you and me?"

"And our desires."

Our desires. He thinks I want to give him some, and he's right. "I would go, but I am not sure about my mama. She might come early."

"My brother's window faces the theater. We will see every car that pulls up. And nothing will happen except for what we both want to happen."

Talking into each other's ears like this is very intimate. Thank goodness for unruly kids.

"What do you want to happen?" I ask.

"I want to show you how I feel about you." He strokes my cheek while he's talking in my ear, and that makes the back of my legs and toes tingle.

"No, what you want to do is feel on me. So, what do you think I want to happen?"

"I think we both know we are only half a step away from love, and I think we both are ready to take that half a step."

"Are you telling me that if I go across the street with you, we will fall in love?" I'm looking at him intently since he is lying, because a smart girl learns a liar's face for future reference.

"No. What I'm saying is there is an opportunity for us to make love, and perhaps us making love will makes us fall in love."

He nibbles on my ear. And now I feel the tingle from the back of my legs rise up my spine and spread across my shoulders. I'm going, but not because of the stupid mess that just came out of his mouth. We're going because this girl has wanted to do it with him a long time, and my body is tired of waiting. I turn to tell Carlos what's up, but he has left the lobby area.

Smiling back to Samuel I say, "Come on."

Chapter Three

Samuel is sweaty wet and lying on top of me like he is about to pass out. This grown man has just popped off for the second time, and neither time did he pull his big ding-a-ling out like he promised. No problem though because I am on the pill, but he doesn't know that, and once he got started he didn't care. And while he was doing what he was doing, I didn't care too much either because of how he was doing what he was doing.

At first, it didn't feel good, and I started not to do it. His ding-a-ling is almost too big, but he squirted a lot of baby oil on it, and I mean a lot, and then it went inside and felt much better. It started feeling so good that my thinking got all jumbled up. My brain told me he was supposed to pull out, but my pussycat wouldn't let my hands push him off. My pussycat wanted him doing what he was doing just like he was doing it.

I do want him to roll off me now though, but I'm too tired to budge. He's not the only one sweaty wet, tired, and blowing long, satisfied breaths.

He rolls off of me and lays his head on the one pillow with me. He has pretty eyelashes, and they are longer than mine. "May, whatever you need, baby, and I mean whatever, whenever, if you need something, baby, just let me know. I swear to God if I weren't married I would marry you today. I want to wake up to you every morning. Watch what I tell you, girl. I'm going to figure this out. We are going to be man and wife. You are my soul mate. Whatever you need, baby, I got it or will get it."

The sex was definitely worth taking the risk of not being at the theater when Mama pulls up. He made me feel that shiver from the inside out a bunch of times. I would have been cool with just the good feelings, but since he's talking that "whatever I need" stuff it's time to tell him what I need, but I have to do it quick because Mama will pull up to the theater in a minute.

"Are you serious about helping me with what I need?" I move my fingers lightly up and down his clammy back. His neck smells like the Gucci counter at Macy's.

"I am your man now, baby. I have to take care of you. You mine."

"You my man?"

"That's right baby. I'm yours, and you mine."

"For real?"

"Baby, it's me and you 'til the end." He kisses me—no tongue, just puckered lips—but I like the feel of it.

"Then since you my man, I'm going to tell you what I need, and if you can't do it just tell me. I know what I am asking is a big deal because my mama can't even do it."

"What is it, baby? What do you need? Tell your man. Tell your man what you need."

I inhale a long breath through my nose because I don't want him to hear me taking it. I say, "I need three hundred dollars to pay my senior fees and get my prom dress. Can you help me with that? Mama just told me yesterday she didn't know how she was going to pay the fees or get the dress. If you give me the money, I'll tell her the school waived my fees and that my friend Michelle will make my dress. If you can do that, I won't have to worry about anything." I keep my eyes on his because he is not looking away. "And the best part is that since I will be buying a dress, I won't have to be over at Michelle's getting fitted for a dress. My dress fitting time will be our time. I can see you during the time I am supposed to be going over Michelle's to get fitted for the dress."

I lay my arm across his shoulder and kiss him. I don't know where the plan came from. It just popped up in my head, but it sounds good to me. "And if I have the money before Mama picks me up, I can tell her all this today, and she can meet Michelle. Can you give me the money before we go back to the theater?"

He blinks his pretty eyes one, two, three, four, five, six times, and says, "Three hundred, huh? I only have a hundred on me."

"Three hundred is what I need from my man." *The proof is in the pudding.* That's what my mama says.

He smiles and puckers for a kiss. I give him one.

"Okay, baby, let me run downstairs to the 7-Eleven. They got a cash machine down there. If it works, you'll have what you need. If not, you'll have to put things on hold until the morning."

"I don't think it will work tomorrow. Today, Michelle will be there to tell Mama that I have to come by her house for the fittings. If we wait until later, Mama will want to talk to Michelle's mama and all that."

"Yeah, I can see that," he says. He rolls out of the sleeper sofa. He rises up, kisses me, and slides into his clothes and out the door.

This will be the most money a boy ever gave me, but, that's right, I keep forgetting Samuel is a man.

His brother lives in what Samuel calls a studio apartment. It's just one room and a bathroom. We did our thing on a pullout sofa. And when Samuel opened the door to go to 7-Eleven, I had to pull the covers over me so no one passing in the hall would see me naked. This studio is not a cool way to live.

Before I can get completely dressed, Samuel is back with fifteen crisp twenty-dollar bills. He wants to fool around some more, and I do too.

But I tell him, "Mama might already be down there. If we stay up here and do it some more and wind up late, she's not going to listen to anything I say. And if I walk up late with you, it's all over. If we want the prom dress thing with Michelle to work, I have to be inside the theater when she pulls up." I put my hand in his pants and wrap my fingers around his thick ding-a-ling. "We can do it again next week and the weeks after if we are smart today."

He blows a heavy sigh. "You're right. I am the one who should be thinking how you're thinking."

***

When I get back to the theater, the play is still in progress, and since it's mostly little kids in the audience, the usher lets me go into the auditorium. I find a seat in the back row and sit down. I pull out my purse and count the fifteen twenty-dollar bills again. Around Samuel, I could not act as excited as I really am. I acted grateful, but not thrilled about the money. This girl is thrilled. Counting the bills again, I let out a little squeal.

"Three hundred dollars!"

I fold the bills and try to think of a place to keep them, a safe place, until I can get home and hide them. Dudes around here snatch purses, and I'd have to cut a thug to the bone for taking this purse. I slip the money into my bra under my right breast. It's a little bigger than the left one, and the money will stay under it.

When I look to the stage, the actors are taking their final bows, the lights come on, and the play is over. The kids are clapping, so they must have enjoyed themselves. I spot Carlos and Michelle sitting low in their theater seats all hugged up. The two teachers are standing up before the kids. One comes to the back by me, and the kids begin to line up behind her. The other teacher stays at the front. The kids have settled down, a lot, and the line is actually orderly as they pass out of the auditorium into the lobby.

Michelle and Carlos are behind the other teacher walking slowly up the center aisle.

"Did you enjoy it?" Michelle asks me.

"Oh, yeah, it was the bomb." I'm talking about Samuel, not the play. I stand from my seat and join them behind the line of children.

"Hey, Michelle, I need to talk to you about something. Didn't I hear girls at school talking about you sewing?"

She nods her head. "Mm-hmm, I sew."

Following them out of the auditorium, I notice her belt is dangling from her jeans belt loop. I tug it, and the belt slides out of the loops. We all stop.

"Oh, my, what were you two doing?"

"Not as much as you," Carlos says. "At least we were at the play."

Blushing, Michelle reaches for her belt and makes a spry break to the bathroom. I decide not to follow her because I want to tell Carlos about the $300. We walk to the front of the ticket window as the children and teachers continue out.

"So where did you and ol' boy go? And I do mean old boy." By the size of the grin on his face, he thinks he has said something clever.

"We went across the street to his brother's place, but, listen to this, he gave me three hundred dollars."

Carlos, who was leaning on the counter of the ticket window, stands erect. He looks like a pigeon just pooped on his shoulder. "For what?" he asks. "Men don't just give women money like that. You need to give him every penny back because whatever he wants you to do, you ain't ready for. God only knows what he wants done for three hundred dollars."

His shocked expression has changed. The look on his face now reminds me of the time Papa pulled me off the curb when a motorcycle ran up in our yard. That was the first and only time I saw Papa scared.

I want to put Carlos at ease, but all there is to say is, "He gave me the money because I told him I needed it for school and for prom."

"Don't he know your mama is going to pay for all that?" he asks in a low tone.

"No, because that's not his business. His business is what I tell him."

He's shaking his head from side to side. "You sound like your mama talking about one of her friends. May, please tell me that man didn't give you three hundred dollars. Let me see it."

He's right. I did sound like my mama, and I'm not sure I like that.

"Let me see, May," he demands actually reaching for my purse.

I pull the purse away but step closer to him so we can continue talking in hushed tones. "I'll show it to you later, but what I want to know is, do you think Michelle will go along with a lie? I need her to tell Mama she is sewing a prom dress for me."

"Have her sew the dress for you and you won't be lying."

"No. I am going to use the time when I'm supposed to be getting my dress sewn to be with Samuel."

"What? You ain't fixin' to pull my girl in on all that mess," he says, no longer whispering.

"What? Your girl? Man, less than two hours ago you were about to dump her butt because you thought she was bald-headed."

"Sssh!" He puts his long index finger to his thick lips. He wants to whisper again.

"Now you worried about me pulling her into some mess? Get real, Carlos. I need you thinking like your normal self. Not like a boy who just got a good blowjob."

His mouth drops open. "How did you know that?" His face is covered with wonderment as if I just figured out the solution to world hunger.

"Focus, Carlos. Will she go for it?"

"Tell me how you knew she did that, and I'll try to focus."

"It's a girl thing. Focus on what I am asking you now, please."

"Tell me!" he says in a whispered shout.

"Fine, it was a simple observation. There was only so much she could do for you in a theater seat, and since you didn't have an erection when you came walking up the aisle, you must have been satisfied. And since there was no wet spot or a dried spot where a wet spot should have been had she given you a hand job, she obviously didn't do that. Hand jobs leave a mess. There is no way around it. No mess, no hand job, but you are satisfied, so she must have given you some head, and since you are now referring to her as 'your girl,' I can only assume that the head was good to you, and that she not only satisfied you but she must have also impressed you by swallowing."

"Ugh! That's nasty. She didn't swallow it. She had some tissue from the bathroom. You must be part witch to figure all that out," he says with no humor in his voice.

I would comment on the witch reference, but Michelle and my little scheme are on my mind. "Now will you focus on my question, please?"

He takes a couple of aimless steps in front of the ticket office, hunches his shoulders, and rubs the fussy hairs on his chin. He looks at me earnestly. "I don't know because that will involve her mama lying too if you supposed to be over their house. Why don't you just ask Michelle can she do the dress without all the other stuff? If she says yes, you can go from there. One step at a time makes a plan."

I give him a big grin. "That's my boy."

Michelle walks up on us still looking a little sheepish. "I think your mama is parked outside. A lady who looks an awful lot like you is standing in front of a black Mustang."

"That's my mama. Hey, Michelle, do you think you can make my prom dress? I can come over once a week for a couple weeks until it's finished, if that's how it's done."

My request must please her because she starts smiling from ear to ear. "Sure, I would love to. Do you have a pattern in mind? If not, don't worry. We can design one. That's what I'm doing with the other girls. I have about five girls coming over on Tuesday and Wednesday evenings, so either one of those days will be fine. And plan on the first couple of visits taking the most time, but after that how much time you spend is up to you."

Another group of kids exit the theater and are heading directly toward us. We start walking toward the exit. I am between her and Carlos.

"Wow, you design, too? I'm going to tell my mama that we will be starting next week. Hey, don't mention a price to her. I'll take care of all that."

I want to stop them both from walking toward the door, so I can nail down the plan, but they are keeping pace with the little kids.

"Okay, but I am very affordable. Your biggest cost will be the material because I don't do much of the sewing. I teach you how to do that."

A breeze blows through the lobby, and when I look to the door, I see my mama coming in. *Dang.* She's looking at her fox jacket, and the smile on her face is not warm, but she seldom snaps on me in public. She has on her long black leather trench with matching leather boots and cap. She could have on a housecoat under it, or she could be dressed.

Quickly I say, "We were just about to come outside to you. I want you to meet a friend of mine. Ma, this is Michelle. Michelle, this is my mama. And, Mama, she sews. She's going to help me make my prom dress."

Still smiling my mama extends her hand to Michelle. "It's good to meet you, young lady."

My mama steps aside, and the little kids go around us and out the other door. To Michelle, my mama says, "I need a new seamstress, so if I like what you do for my daughter I'll be checking you out."

Shaking my mama's hand, Michelle answers, "Like I was telling May, what I do is teach others how to sew. When we are done, she will be a good seamstress. She should be able to do most of your sewing."

My mama huffs, "Mm, hope I live to see it. And what's wrong with you, Carlos, cat got your tongue? When did you stop speaking to me?"

"Ah, no, Ms. Joyce," he says. "It's not like that." He bends to kiss her on the cheek. "I was waiting for you to finish talking."

"Now, boy, you have known me all your life. You know I am never finished talking. Come on, May, we got to get on back home. Your uncle Doug is back in town."

That means her friend Doug must have found another job. He probably came over with a pocket full of cash and a bottle, and Mama is more than likely working the cash out of his pocket bit by bit. First, she will hit him with her needs. Then, she will probably tell him about me being a senior and all the fees associated with that, and next will be the house and her car. That conversation will go on and on until more friends come over, and then the card games will start. Her other friends will leave in the wee hours of the morning, and then she and Doug will go into her bedroom where the bulk of what remains in his pocket will be left behind.

I think about the $300 in my bra and Carlos saying I sound like my mother. I don't want to be like my mama, but I do want the $300. My happy feeling about the money is changing, a little. But, I'm still happy.

As we all are exiting the theater Carlos says, "Hey, don't forget about Walter. He's supposed to have a pair of gym shoes for me, too."

I had forgotten about Walter with Mama's upcoming party on my mind. The house is going to be loud all night and, since she will be entertaining people, I will have to mind the back door for our after-hours business. If I go home and go to sleep now, when she starts calling me around three in the morning, I will have gotten a little rest. I really don't have time for slow-acting Walter tonight, new gym shoes or not.

"Hey, why don't you come over and sit with him for an hour and a half and talk about old movies and comic books?" I ask Carlos.

"Naw, you got that. Ah, shoot, that's right. I do have a *Fantastic Four* piece for him that my mama ordered, so I will stop by." He lowers his voice to a whisper, and to the back of my neck he says, "And I want to see what ol' boy gave you."

Once we get in the parking lot, my mama walks ahead of us to her car.

"All that ain't your business," I say to him in regard to Samuel's gift.

"What did you say?"

"You heard me. You can come see Walter, but everything else you talking about is you being nosey. You're trying to put your nose into grown folks' business."

"Yeah, right. You ain't grown. Messing with an old-ass man don't make you grown. See you tonight."

"Michelle, ain't you got something for your man to do that will keep him out of my business?"

She answers me with giggles as Carlos holds open the Cadillac door for her.

Chapter Four

Mama has two other friends and Uncle Doug at her party. There are four old folks in total and me and Walter in the kitchen. Mama and her friends are in the front room, and thank goodness there is a dining room between us because Uncle Doug's blues music is really getting on my nerves. He is playing it as loud as he plays his gospel music on Sunday mornings when he stays over. And he is playing the spit-hacking, throat-clearing, and countrified Bobby Blue Bland, the worst one out of all his blues singers as far as I am concerned. But, to Uncle Doug, Bobby Blue Bland is the "man."

I think Uncle Doug likes him the best because people say they sound the same when talking, and Uncle Doug can mimic his singing to a T. With the kitchen door closed, the real Bobby Blue Bland and Uncle Doug are both muffled. Now, if I could only muffle Walter.

He has been trying to get downstairs to the recreation room, but that is not happening. I am glad he is here, though. I have to man the back door for the store when she has a party, so I don't get any sleep. When Walter texted me to come over, I told him to come around two this morning, and he did. I would not have done that for him, but he has been begging me to sneak downstairs since he's been here. And I keep telling him that's not happening.

My pussycat is finished getting petted for the evening. Matter of fact, she is finished for the rest of the month. I never do it more than once a month. My vagina is not going to get stretched all out of shape. I'm not sure if it's having babies, or too many ding-a-lings, or age that causes a pussycat to get stretched out all big, and I don't want to find out.

Carlos told me he did it to a girl on the beach last summer, and her pussycat was so big that he just went right into her with no type of resistance, and he said he could barely feel her insides because nothing gripped his ding-a-ling. He said it was like he stuck his ding-a-ling in a bowl of warm, soupy oatmeal. I wondered how he knew what it felt like to stick his ding-a-ling in a bowl of oatmeal, but I didn't ask. No way am I going to let my pussycat get it into that kind of shape.

And he said that the girl was a senior last year at Calumet. That means, at the most, she is only two years older than me.

The only time sex really gets on my mind is right before my menstrual. The few times I have done it was before my period. Other than that, a boy can beg until he is blue in the face and balls, but it's not happening unless I feel like it, and I only feel it when the boy is totally into me.

Walter was the first person I did it with, and we have done it three times since then. I chose him because I was certain he wouldn't tell anyone about it, and he hasn't. He didn't even tell Carlos. At least to my knowledge he hasn't. Besides, if he did tell, no one would believe a girl as fine as me gave it to a nerd like him. He's still shocked over it.

I have done it with two others boys besides Walter. We were on vacation in Florida last summer, and I met this boy named Andy. A beautiful half-Greek, half-black boy who told me he had prayed to meet a girl like me. He swore it was love at first sight for him. We did it on his grandfather's rooftop under a sky filled with stars. The other boy was Quincy. He wrote me thirty-seven love poems, made fifteen mix tapes, took me to his family reunion in Gary, Indiana, and bought me a gold and cubic zirconia bracelet that he sold his mountain bike to get. We were alone in his basement after his father's funeral when I decided to give him some. He was so sad, but not afterward, which made me feel pretty good.

The three other times Walter and I did it were by default. Once, I was mad at a boyfriend. The next time, I was a little tipsy and it was close to my monthly, and our last fling was Christmas. He gave me my first real Gucci bag, and I was happy about it, so I took him down to the recreation room and gave him some, but tonight I am not tipsy, and the Nikes he bought me are not a Christmas gift, and my mind is on Samuel.

That man made me feel good this afternoon. Imagine a grown man like him wanting me as bad as he does. He told me if he were not married he would marry me, and I believe him, too.

Whatever I need, he said he would get it because he is my man, not my boyfriend, my man. I told him what I needed, and he gave it to me: $300. And he gave me the money after we made love, so it's not about him trying to get something out of me like Carlos was saying.

My fine grown man has a thing for me, and I got a thing for him too. He is one good-looking man who knows how to do it. I know looks aren't everything, but they sure help. Samuel makes me like to think about having sex. When I hear his deep bass voice, and when I watch him walk, and when the man kisses me, I catch on fire. No begging boy has ever made me feel like he does.

Begging boys are annoying. Walter is a begging boy, and right now he is very, very annoying. Maybe if he were half as fine as Samuel he would stand a chance. I remember when Papa showed me the meaning of the word "fine."

We were at a Saturday morning Operation Push meeting. He and I went to park the car while Mama and Grandma went inside the building. By the time we got back all the seats were filled, so Papa and I stood along the side wall of the hall. While standing there, he told me to look through the crowd and see if I could find any women prettier than my mama and Grandma. I tried my best because I was mad at them for not saving us a seat, but there wasn't a prettier woman present.

"The only person in here as fine as them is you. You come from beautiful people. Don't ever forget that May, never."

I didn't think too much of what he was saying back then because I was only about eight, and now I don't think too much about it because the boys won't let me forget. If I weren't attractive, Samuel wouldn't have looked at me twice, and if he weren't fine, I wouldn't have looked at him once. Those green eyes of his send me off to dreamland every time. If I could change anything about him, I would make him a couple of shades darker with the same eyes. Darker men look tougher, harder. Not that Samuel is soft, because he's not. It's just that he would look better darker. Walter's Tootsie Roll brown color would look good on Samuel.

Lord knows Walter would never let me forget I am attractive. He has written dozens of poems about my beauty, he buys me greeting cards that profess it, and he tells me every time he sees me how fine I am. Especially when he wants to do it like he does now. When he is in this state, I can make him do almost anything with only the slightest sexual reward.

The punishment my mama assigned for me wearing her fox jacket without asking was scrubbing the back hall walls along with mopping the bathroom and kitchen floors. Since she and her company are up front, I was able to get Walter to do the punishment chores for me, and all I had to do was let him suck my breasts for a little while. Boys are stupid, but horny boys are very stupid.

The only boy I know who doesn't tell me how good I look all the time is Carlos, but I don't tell him how good he looks either. I really didn't notice his looks until other girls started pointing them out. Once, when we were kids, I told Mama Carlos was my boyfriend. Man, she flipped out. She called Ms. Carol over and everything.

The two of them sat Carlos and me down and told us we were like brother and sister and could never play boyfriend and girlfriend. They told us that playing brother and sister was way better than boyfriend and girlfriend, and they took us to McDonald's to prove it. "See, brothers and sisters can do all kind of fun things together," one of them had said.

That was one of the few times I can remember my mama and Ms. Carol coming together on something. They are usually at odds. Each of them rolling their eyes and smacking their lips at the sight of the other. When I was younger, I thought they disliked each other because my mama had left the water hose on one day and drowned all of Ms. Carol's roses, but I now know their battle started before Carlos or I was born.

Walter is getting on my last nerve begging to go downstairs. *Good, somebody is ringing the back doorbell.* Looking up at the clock I see it's three-fifteen. The liquor store on the corner closed about fifteen minutes ago. People are going to start coming over.

It's not a customer at the door. It's Carlos and Michelle, and Michelle looks like she's been crying. I let them walk in without asking questions. Although I have a bunch of them like, why is Carlos out at three-fifteen in the morning when his mama still enforces a strict one a.m. curfew, even on weekends? And what happened to make Michelle look like she has pink eye in both eyes?

I let them sit at my mama's new blond oak kitchen table, and I pour them both some of my hot chocolate, made from milk, not water, before I ask, "So what the hell happened?"

Michelle starts crying out loud, and Carlos pulls her head to his shoulder. Walter moves the coffee mugs out of the way. He puts them both in front of me instead of taking them to the sink. *Stupid.*

"Her mama," Carlos begins. "We got in kind of late, and her mama snapped, called us both all kinds of names. Then she called the police and told them I raped Michelle. She tried to make me stay there until the police came. Statutory rape is what she kept screaming, said I was too old to be going out with Michelle. She's crazy. We are the same age.

"I just raised up out of there, and Michelle followed me. After driving around awhile and not being able to figure nothing out I called my mom, but Michelle's mama had already called her and filled her head with all kinds of mess. My mom told me to take Michelle to the hospital and have the doctors check her out if I didn't rape her. She told me I couldn't come home until it was all straightened out. Michelle didn't want to go to the hospital because we have been getting busy, and she said the doctor would be able to tell that she is not a virgin."

Hold it. Did he say virgin? "Wait, you gave your virginity to him?" I ask Michelle while pointing to Carlos with my thumb.

My question makes her cry more. Carlos looks at me as if I just slapped an infant and he grunts out, "Hey, her giving it to me is better than you giving yours to Walter." He doesn't say it loud. It is plainly stated, but the words sound off and echo in my head. I turn my gaze to Walter.

"I didn't tell him. I swear," he mouths in a whisper.

From him, my eyes go to Michelle then back to Carlos who has a stomach-twisting smirk on his face. "You just told me, May," he says looking directly into my eyes. "Guess I ain't as dumb as you think, huh?"

Oh, I hate him, and I am about to tell him just how much, but my heart starts beating loud in my head, so loud that I cannot get my mind around what I want to say to him. Under the kitchen table, I feel Walter's hand grabbing a hold of my hand. I hold on. I hold on tight to Walter's hand, and I breathe. Exhaling along with squeezing his hand is calming me down.

Clinging to Walter feels good. Now, isn't that strange?

Okay, there must be something I can say to Carlos to get that smug look off his face. It's kind of weird because even though he has that dang smirk on his face, his eyes are still sad. The situation he and Michelle are in has really gotten to him and has him acting out of character. I'm going to be the bigger person. Besides, I am not the type of girl who would kick a dog when it's hurting, never mind my best friend.

I decide to say nothing mean. What I say is, "If you wanted to know about my virginity all you had to do was ask me. I'm not bashful about anything I do."

Carlos looks away. The kitchen is quiet. I grab the mugs from the table, stand, and take them to the sink.

When I sit back down Michelle says, "I love Carlos. Sharing myself with him was what was supposed to happen. Of that, I am certain. From the first day my eyes saw him, my heart knew he was the one."

In my whole life, I have never heard a black girl say anything as corny as that.

Blues music floods the kitchen, and we all look to the opening door and see Uncle Doug two-step through it. "How all y'all doin'?" His eyes are glossy and red, and his face is flushed. Uncle Doug and I share the same complexion, and we both flush easily.

What has always confused me about Uncle Doug is the way he dresses. He wears what Mama calls slacks: thick polyester dress pants with a waistband. I have never seen these pants in any stores, but he always has on a new-looking pair, and the colors range from rust to sky blue, no grays, no blacks, no navy blues. Lime green, burnt orange, maroon, purple, and white are his choices. His shirts are just as much a mystery: shiny nylon with long collars, and they too always look new. Carlos calls his shoes roach killers because of the pointy toes. He says even if a roach ran in the corner, Uncle Doug would be able to smash it with the pointy toe of his patent leather shoes. Tonight, his roach killers are black, his slacks are red, and his nylon shirt with the long collar is black and red. A hot mess in my opinion, but Uncle Doug thinks he is fly or "sharp as a tack," as he says.

"May, ya mama said give me that half a bag of ice out the top of the box," Uncle Doug says pushing his thin, straight black hair back out of his eyes. Mama says he uses a soup bowl to cut his hair. He puts the bowl on his head and cuts every hair that hangs past the bowl, and I can see that looking at his head.

The back doorbell rings as Uncle Doug is asking me for the ice. Without me asking him, Walter stands and goes over to the refrigerator. He opens the freezer compartment and pulls out the bag of ice while I go to the back door. Uncle Doug comes and gets the ice, and does a dance step right back out the door, pulling it closed and muffling the blues again.

At the back door are two regular customers. One wants a fifth of red Richards Wild Irish Rose, and the other wants a forty ounce of Olde English malt liquor. Walter opens the bottom half of the refrigerator and pulls out both orders. He hands them to me, and I walk back over to the door and serve the customers. I lock the door and turn around to see a curious look on Michelle's face.

"Yeah?" I query.

"Where is your food kept, if the refrigerator is filled with drinks and ice?"

Sitting back at the table I ask, "Girl, with everything you dealing with tonight that's what you got on your mind?"

"Yes. I know, but I have always been eccentric with the timing of my questions. I get that from my mama. So, where is your food?"

"We have a refrigerator and deep freezer in the basement."

"Oh," she says and then goes silent.

To my best friend I say, "You want me to call your mama? Sometimes she listens to me more than you."

Looking at Michelle but talking to me he answers, "Yeah, I think that's a good idea. Either you or your mama."

"My mama?" Dang, the boy really is mixed up in the head.

"Yeah, you right, not your mama. You better call her."

My friend is in a peculiar state. Seldom are his statements useless or pointless, and I can count the times on one hand when his head has been lowered as it is now. Michelle is not the girl for him. She is putting him through too much already.

"Maybe you could call my mama too. No, not my mama. My father. Call my house and ask for my father. If you can speak to him, he will talk to my mama and get her straight." Michelle's face brightens some. "Matter of fact, I am sure that's what you should do. No, not you. I will call."

I'm glad she corrected that because there is no way I am calling her family's house this time of morning. The back doorbell rings again. Walter and I stand up at the same time.

"I got it," I say.

He sits back down but keeps his eyes on me as I walk to the door. Looking out the peephole, I see Ms. Carol.

"Dang, it's your mama," I say to Carlos, and I open the door without hesitation.

She walks right in. She has on a pink house-coat and a pair of Carlos's gym shoes. She had to be freezing out there. Ms. Carol is a tall woman, but she is very thin. She has no meat to protect her against the cold.

"Damn!" Ms. Carol has a big, dog-barking voice like Carlos's. "I don't know what was on my mind coming over here without a coat," she says and immediately closes the door behind her.

Everyone at the table stands when she enters. She rubs her hands together and does a blood-cir-culating dance for warmth. When she stops, her eyes are on Michelle.

"Your parents are on their way over here."
Looking at Carlos she says, "You two might as
well sit back down. You are not to leave. And
don't even think about driving my car ever again.
You will be thirty before I trust you with another
car of mine." To me, she says, "I need to speak
to Gloria."

Now, this could be a situation. I cannot
remember Ms. Carol ever being in our house.
"Wait here a moment please."

Ms. Carol takes my seat at the table. Walter
nods toward the door. I don't blame him. If I
could leave, I would.

"Carlos, would you lock the door behind
Walter?"

Walking through the door into the dining
room, I take a very large breath to get ready for
what could be an explosion.

Chapter Five

Mama and Uncle Doug are sitting together on the sofa watching her other two guests dance. Stepping, they call it. I walk to Mama and bend to her ear and whisper, "Ms. Carol is in the kitchen, and she needs to explain something to you."

I thank God that Mama isn't drunk, her eyes are clear and focused, and she understands what I have said. She stands. "Excuse me for a minute, y'all."

While walking through the dining room, Mama stops us by the cherry wood breakfront. "Now what's going on in here? Doug told me you have company, too."

"It's just Walter, Carlos, and his new girlfriend, Michelle." I totally understand the stern look she gives me. Three people is not "just." "Just" would have been only Walter, or only Carlos. "Well, it was just Walter, but Carlos and Michelle came over unexpected."

"And why is Carol in my house?"

"Carlos and Michelle got in trouble with Michelle's mama and Ms. Carol. They came over here to sort things out. Ms. Carol must have seen her car parked in front of our house and guessed that Carlos was here. She came over to make sure they didn't leave before Michelle's parents come over."

Mama presses her thin lips together and says, "This sounds like a situation that should be handled at her house, not mine."

She's right. "I know, Mama, but this is where it all came together. I think Ms. Carol was afraid Carlos and Michelle wouldn't stay put long enough for her parents to get here."

Mama sucks her teeth. "That's a lot of nerve. The woman knows what is going on at my house this time of night. I bet she wouldn't have this going on at her house during one of her crap games. And we don't even know what type of people the girl's parents are. One of them could be the police for all we know. No, they're going to have deal with this at her house."

Mama has been bootlegging for so long that most times I forget it's illegal to sell liquor after hours from a home without a license. It's second nature to me. I sell beer and icy cups just the same.

"How soon will the girl's parents be here?"

"I don't know, Mama."

She walks ahead of me into the kitchen. When we enter and we hear, "That's a brand-new Cadillac, and you disappear in it for over sixteen hours, and the only explanation you have is 'you didn't know what to do'? What you should have done is kept your little prick in your pants and brought my damn car home."

"Ma!" Carlos barks.

"Don't 'Ma' me! Shit, you wrong, boy!"

Speaking at a level only I can hear, my mama says, "Okay, for Carlos's sake we will do it here." Louder, she says, "Hey, Carol, it's good to see you, girl. Now you know better than to let these kids stress you out. What's going on here?" She sits in the seat Walter left empty, and that leaves me standing.

"Girl, this boy done went and did it to that child over there," Ms. Carol answers pointing to Michelle. "And now her mama says he raped her, and she's threatening to call the police, but the child don't look traumatized to me. What happened was they just got caught trying to be grown. They went somewhere and stayed gone long enough to have her parents and me walking the floors with worry, and all the boy can say is 'he didn't know what to do.' But they both knew what to do hours ago when they were doing the bump-nasty. And y'all bet' not have been doing it my new Cadillac. It better not smell like sex. Give me my damn keys!"

Carlos pulls the keys from his jacket pocket and hands them to her.

The back doorbell rings. I walk to it and look out the peephole. There are about four customers. I open the door and take their orders: three forty ounces and one fifth of White Rose. I serve them without turning to look at the table. The bootleg money is house spending money and my allowance. We are not going to stop selling.

When I close the back door, the front doorbell rings. Mama stands and walks through the dining room door.

Ms. Carol's hard stare has forced both Carlos's and Michelle's heads down. To me, she says, "I hope you haven't started acting grown, May. Believe me, life has plenty of time for sex once you are an adult. Right now is the time to be thinking about school and your future. All sex will do at this time in your life is get in the way. I been telling you and Carlos that for years. I hope you been listening more than him."

"Yes, ma'am," is my reply.

My mama comes back into the kitchen with Uncle Doug and her other two guests. "May, your uncle Doug is going to answer the back door while we all go up front and speak with Michelle's father."

Uncle Doug and the other two guests sit in the chairs we leave empty.

It's Mama, Ms. Carol, Michelle, Carlos, Michelle's daddy, and me all in the living room. Michelle's daddy and Ms. Carol have taken the easy chairs. The rest of us—Carlos, Mama, Michelle, and I—are on the couch.

Mama's newly painted ivory walls look dingy white to me with Ms. Carol and Mr. Pickens looking all around. Nothing in the living room seems up to par under their glance: the cocktail and end tables are dusty, the lamps are old-fashioned, the pattern of big flowers on the couch and easy chairs, which I originally thought comfortable and homey, now look country and backward, especially when I think about Ms. Carol's leather living room furniture. Even Mama in her short blue jean skirt and lace-up halter top seem inappropriate with them here.

Looking at Michelle's father, Mr. Pickens, I see he hasn't changed too much from when Carlos and I were in his acting program. He's still slim, and he still keeps his black wavy hair cut close. He has the blackest eyes that I have ever seen in my life. When I was a kid, I thought it was because the whites of his eyes were so bright, but both parts of his eyes are intense. The whites are as pure as a glass of milk, and the black part is as dark as one of Grandma's cast-iron skillets.

Mr. Pickens is the first to speak. "Okay, before we get started, I want to say what a pleasant surprise it is to see you again, May, despite the circumstances. May, you were a very good actor. I hope you are still pursing the craft in some form. You brought the house down in *The Lion King*. Yes, it was a couple of years ago, but your performance is still remembered. I could use you as senior youth coach. The position pays, so think about," he says staring right at me.

Acting was cool, but that was kid stuff. But he did say it paid. "Thank you, Mr. Pickens. Senior youth coach, huh? At Foster Park?" I ask.

"Yep, the program is housed there now. That is our central office. Are you interested?"

"I think I am," I say smiling at him. And I am interested. Being at the theater earlier has me reminiscing about acting. Moving my eyes from Mr. Pickens to my mama, I see she is smiling, and that makes me happy. I like making my mama proud.

"Good. We need you there. Okay, that being said, back to the matter at hand. Young man, I have no plans to press any charges against you." Mr. Pickens is looking real hard at Carlos. "My wife was worried to the point of being hysterical. You and my daughter were very inconsiderate in your actions today."

He turns toward his daughter and says, "Michelle, due to what we all think occurred and has been occurring, you will take a pregnancy test, and this will put all the adult minds to rest. At this juncture, I personally don't want to hear any comments from either of you. The situation speaks for itself." His intense eyes go back and forth from Michelle to Carlos.

Dang, I think it's a little extreme him not giving them an opportunity to say a thing in their defense, but it's cool of him to say his wife was tripping, and that they are not pressing any charges against Carlos. I know Ms. Carol is glad to hear that.

To her, he says, "Carol, I will notify you of the results of the pregnancy test later this morning. I believe we can all use some—"

He didn't finish his sentence because some dudes have busted through the dining room door. One has a pistol to Uncle Doug's head. Two others are pushing Mama's guests through the door. Uncle Doug and the other guests are slung to the floor at our feet.

The three dudes have on stocking-cap masks. Their faces are all smashed and contorted. But their clothes and builds are familiar. I think I know these dudes.

"Everybody empty dey pockets and remove all y'all jewelry."

That sounds like Mooky. No one moves until he fires a shot up into the ceiling. Plaster dust is falling all around us. Ms. Carol screams, and so does Mama's lady guest.

"I mean right now!"

That floor-creaking voice can only belong to Mooky. I'll bet anything. Mama hasn't budged. She is staring hard at Mooky too.

Dang, that gunshot has it smelling like firecrackers in here. The second dude comes around with an orange Aldi bag for us to start dumping our stuff in. It's Blake with the bag. His blue and white North Carolina Hornets jacket is a dead giveaway. He was in the same class with Carlos, Edith, and me until the seventh grade, when he got shipped to a "bad boy" school down state.

The $300 I got from Samuel is in my bra. I have no plans of giving it to them. I pull off my two gold rings and the gold link chain from around my neck. Mr. Pickens removes his wallet from his hip pocket and removes a stack of twenties and dumps them into the bag.

Ms. Carol drops a gold chain and one ring, and Carlos pulls his wallet from his hip pocket. He has one ten-dollar bill, and from his front pants pocket he pulls some loose singles and change. Michelle gets her wallet from her purse, and she has a couple singles and a five.

Mama has on three diamond rings, and she has made no move to remove them.

Mooky says, "Take off the rings, bitch."

"Don't talk to my mama like that, Mooky!"

"Ho, you don't know me."

"I do know you. Everybody in here knows it's you. Y'all ain't fooling nobody: Mooky, Blake, and Drake. Now what? We all know who you are. What, you going to rob us and then shoot us?"

He ignores me and to Mama says, "I ain't tellin' you again. Take off the rings."

"I don't think so," Mama says. "Your friend has my cash box under his arm. It's over two hundred dollars in there. That's all you gettin' from me."

The third dude, Drake, does have our cash box, dang.

When Mooky steps toward Mama, Uncle Doug jumps up from the floor and punches him straight in the jaw. Carlos leaps from the couch and throws Grandma's crystal lamp at the second dude, Blake, knocking him back. Carlos follows the lamp and starts beating Blake down. Then Drake tries to move toward Carlos, but Mr. Pickens trips him, and when he falls Mr. Pickens starts stomping him in the head.

Mama reaches under the couch cushion. I know she is feeling for one of her pistols. She gets it and shoots Mooky in the leg. He topples over and drops his gun. Uncle Doug picks it up and pulls the trigger, but the gun doesn't fire.

Mama orders the other to dudes to stop moving. They try to, but Carlos and Mr. Pickens are beating them. She screams, "Carlos, Mr. Pickens, stop!"

Carlos stops, but Mr. Pickens stomps Drake in the head one more time and says, "Punk-ass motherfucker."

Dang, Mr. Pickens went straight gangster.

Mama orders the other two dudes to lie down next to the one she shot. Once they crawl over here, I rip off their stocking-cap masks. I knew it was them: Drake, a buster who will follow anybody doing anything; Blake, the neighborhood crackhead; and the one Mama shot is Mooky, who used to be a big shot.

Uncle Doug has all their guns, and none of them have any shells except for the spent one in Mooky's gun. They tried to rob us with one bullet. Mama goes through their pockets and gets seven dollars, total.

She picks her cash box up from the floor. The money is still in there. She adds the seven dollars and tells me, "Get them three bottles of Richards red. Doug and Carlos, put these broke-ass niggas out the back door."

I hurry to the kitchen to get the three bottles of wine and to get the back door open, but the door is still open from when they forced their way in. I'm certain Mama isn't going to call the police. She knows Blake's and Mooky's mamas, but the main reason she doesn't call is because she doesn't want the police in our house. Mama thinks if the police find out about her selling after-hours liquor she would have to give them a cut of what she takes in. Personally, I think the police already know and don't care about our little store.

Uncle Doug and Mr. Pickens have Blake and Drake by their collars. When they pass me, I hand them each a bottle as they are being ushered out the door. Carlos has Mooky, who is limping and bleeding badly. I hand him his wine as Carlos assists him out the door. When he gets to the bottom of the steps, his buddies are there to help him.

Mooky is saying something about getting his guns back, but Carlos slams the door on him. If his guns work, Mama will be adding them to her collection of ten. She says a house with only women needs to be safe. She has at least one gun in every room including the bathrooms. When I was twelve, she took Carlos and me out to the gun range in Indiana and taught us how to shoot, load a gun, and clean it. I am a better shot than her and Carlos.

Standing in front of the closed back door Carlos asks, "Do you believe Mooky and them tried that? What were they thinking? Everybody in the hood knows your mama got more pistols than Kellogg's got flakes. And when I saw his bum-ass gym shoes, I knew it was Blake's thirsty ass, and soon as Mooky opened his mouth I knew it was him. What were they thinking? All of them must be smoking crack with Blake to try something that stupid."

He's probably right. The three of them must be on drugs. No one thinking right would try to rob people who can recognize them. "Hey, where are Mr. Pickens and Uncle Doug?"

"They walked them to the front gate. I guess they gonna come through the front door."

Mama comes into the kitchen. "We are closed until tomorrow night, May. Y'all come on back up front." She hands me my rings and chain and Carlos his cash. Then she reaches under the sink and gets the Pine-Sol and a couple of rags, and from the side of the refrigerator she gets the bucket and fills it with cold water and then she walks up front with us.

Michelle, her father, and Ms. Carol are standing in the vestibule at the door. Uncle Doug is on the couch. The other two guests are gone.

Mr. Pickens walks from the vestibule to my mama and hugs her. "My apologies for my actions. I see now that you had the situation under control."

My mama is caught off guard by his hug. I can tell because she doesn't hug him back. Her arms are dangling at her sides. Her eyes are also blinking nonstop, which is what happens when she is startled.

After he has freed her from the hug, she says, "Oh, no, I had nothing under control. If you all hadn't moved when you did, things could have gone the other way."

For the first time tonight, Ms. Carol laughs. "Yeah, but you weren't giving up those rings, girl. I think you shocked them stupid with your refusal. And your guy leaping up from the floor surely startled them. I'm going home, and I'm thanking the good Lord for making it possible that we can all go home. He's got a way of showing you what is important and what's not. I should have been thankful that my son made it home tonight. He and your daughter, Mr. Pickens, could have been in some ditch, dead. Yes, they were wrong for worrying us, but they're home safe, and that's more important. I will be waiting for your call tomorrow. Come on here, boy. Good night, all."

Michelle leaves through the door without saying a word. She and Carlos exchange a worried look, and both leave with their parents. The only person still here is Uncle Doug. He takes the bucket and the cleaning stuff from Mama and says, "I'll get this blood out of your carpet, Gloria. You go on and rest. I'll let you know when I'm finished, and, if I'm here in the morning, I'll plaster that bullet hole in your ceiling, too."

He is grinning while looking at my mama like she is the apple of his eye, like Papa used to say. I turn my back on both of them and head back to my bedroom.

Chapter Six

I collapse on Grandma and Papa's big sleigh bed. Mama moved it back here when she took their room up front. I got the big bed, but she got the big bedroom. This used to be her room, and when it was hers she had it painted yellow and white. When I moved in, I had her get the walls painted a pastel pink and the ceiling hot pink. Uncle Doug, who painted it, calls my room "Mary Kay Central."

I'm tired of the pinks now. I want an all-tan room because Grandma's winter comforter bedspread is light brown, and the one she used for the spring is beige. None of her bedding matches my pink walls, and now I want to use her bedding with her bed because it will be like having a little bit of her around.

My old room is across the hall. Now, it is the library. Mama put in bookshelves that reach the ceiling, a schoolteacher's desk, and a computer. She filled the shelves with the books Papa had scattered all through the house. He had books stacked in corners, lining the baseboards of the dining room, and on closet shelves. She gathered them all and made a library. Papa read fiction, how-to books, and biographies. He tried to get me to read a couple books by Toni Morrison, but I would rather watch a movie. It's not like I don't read. *Vibe, People, Vogue, Essence* all hold my attention, but books take too much time. I added the magazines to our library.

Reaching into my bra, I pull out the fifteen crisp twenty-dollar bills from Samuel. "Now, that's what I'm talking about." $300 cash. What will I buy? What can I buy that won't get Mama suspicious? Well, first I'm going to replace all my underwear with new, matching sets. The good sets from Lord & Taylor. I would like to get Mama a good set too, but she would ask too many questions: where did I get the money, who gave it to me, and why? And those types of questions would put her deep into my business, but I'm going to buy her a couple sets anyway. I will tell her I got them from a booster or something.

Tomorrow is allowance day, and she knows my plans are to go shopping. I used to go with Edith, but we haven't talked. I need to call her, but she hasn't called me either. I want to talk to her about Samuel, too, but maybe not. Since she's been going to church, our boy conversations have changed. Between my going to a new school and her going to church we barely talk. It's a lot like Mama said: "Life changes your friends."

I'll let Mama think I'm going to the Plaza like usual, but I'll catch the "L" downtown and go to the Water Tower. *Oh, wait, I don't have to catch the "L." My man drives.*

And my man knows how to do it.

That was the best time of my sexual life. I have never shivered from the inside out that many times before, and to think I almost didn't do it because I didn't think we were going to get his ding-a-ling inside me. Grown men do it better than boys, but he was just like a boy not wanting to pull it out. I wonder when all boys get grown if their ding-a-lings grow to be as big as Samuel's. I roll over to my nightstand and reach under the top drawer and untape the pill pack. I pop one out and swallow it dry and tape the pack back under my drawer.

I look at the phone on my nightstand. He never said when I couldn't call him. Saturday, 4:05 a.m., the clock reads. What he said was call him when I thought about him. Well, I'm thinking about him. He might be up, or he might be in bed with his wife, and he might be doing it to her right now. If we were married, he would be doing it to me right now. I wonder if he does it to his wife like he did it to me.

No, he doesn't, because if they did it like we did it, he wouldn't have gotten with me because he would have been satisfied. She met him first. That's why she is his wife. He told me he is going to find a way for us to be together. He said we are soul mates. If they did it like we did it, he wouldn't have said those things to me. It would have been just sex. We made love, just like he said we would.

But, I don't think I love him. I love how we did it, and I really love the money he gave me, but I don't think I love him. We made love, but I don't think I fell in love with him. No, he is not my soul mate, and I certainly wouldn't marry him. I don't even want to see just him, and he certainly is not taking me to my prom.

I think Michelle loves Carlos, but he doesn't love her. If she's pregnant, he's screwed. Ms. Carol will make him marry her. I should call Samuel and tell him I love him just to get inside his head. Uncle Doug loves Mama. He risked taking a bullet for her. He jumped up off the floor and socked Mooky right in the jaw when he made a move toward Mama. I wonder if she would marry Uncle Doug if she could. I think he's married. One day I'm going to ask him and see what he says. If he says he's not married, I'm going to tell him to marry Mama and see how he acts. It would be nice to have a comforter on my bed. This pink thermal blanket gets lint balls in my hair. Mama said she had puppy love for my daddy, but he didn't even have that for her. When I asked her who and where he was, all she said was, "He is a filthy junkie with a needle in his arm who the State couldn't even find. He doesn't give a damn about you or me so don't ask me shit else about him." And I didn't because she made him sound so horrible. Besides, I had Papa, and he was better than any daddy.

I pick up the phone and push in Samuel's seven numbers. He answers alert like he wasn't even asleep.

"Hey, baby, it's May. No, I haven't been to sleep. Some dudes tried to rob the store tonight, but Mama shot one, and the other two got beat down. No, none of us got hurt. Why are you up so early? Every day you have to be there at four in the morning? Yeah, I know school buses are out early, but I didn't think you started to work this early. Oh, since you, like, the boss you got to be there to make sure drivers get out on time, I understand. For real, you been thinking about me? I been thinking about you too. Yeah, you made me feel good. Yeah, special. Yeah, like a queen. Yeah, you my king. Yeah, call me at your break. Maybe today, if you feel like driving downtown to Water Tower—

"You don't love me. Why did you say that? Okay, we will see. Call me on your break. Goodbye."

I don't say "I love you" back to him. Those words can't flow from my mouth like they do from his. So, I guess I want to be playing with his head. He told me he loved me. Maybe he does love me. He ought to. I look way better than his wife.

What I need to do is get up out of this bed, take off these clothes, and head for the shower. But I don't want to hear what Uncle Doug and Mama might be doing, and going all the way downstairs to the bathroom would be a bit much right now.

It bothers me to hear Mama's lovemaking noises ever since I figured out what the noises were. She moans and chirps like a bird when it's good to her. And when she and Uncle Doug get together she goes chirp crazy, and I don't want to hear all that. Besides, I feel the Sandman pulling me right into dreamland. All I have to do is not move.

It's Mama's wedding. Papa and Grandma are here in the backyard, and relatives who haven't been over to the house in years are here. Papa and Grandma are sitting in the front row of white chairs. I can barely see their faces. The backyard is fixed up pretty with white chiffon trails from the chairs, and there is a white gazebo in the middle of the yard. White ribbon is weaved through the chain-link fence, and a path of white carpet leads to the gazebo.

As I walk through the sunny yard, I greet my cousins, aunts, and uncles, but no one answers me. Sitting next to Papa is Uncle Doug and when I look to see who Mama's groom is I see the bride is not Mama anymore but Michelle and the groom is Carlos. The once clear, bright sky becomes overcast, and the wind begins to build up.

A gust of wind whips through the yard turning over chairs, sending church lady hats into flight, and rocking the gazebo. People are fleeing for shelter. I run to Papa and Grandma, but they walk through the back gate, and I can't catch up with them. All of a sudden, the clouds start ringing, and everyone I look at has the same ringing sound coming out of their mouths.

I blink my eyes open to the ringing phone. Looking to the clock, I see it reads Saturday, 6:15

a.m. I pick up the phone and hear crying and sobbing on the other end. The voice says she has missed two periods, and Carlos wants to join the Army and marry her and not go to Ohio State. She wants me to talk to him and tell him not to join the Army, and convince him that going away to school is best.

Neither his nor her parents know she's pregnant, but everyone will know after she takes the pregnancy test. That's what they were doing last night: trying to figure out the right thing to do. Her mama asked her this morning why there were so many tampons left in the box she bought her three months ago. She didn't have an answer for her, so her mama threw the box at her and called her a stupid, selfish child.

She says both she and Carlos want to keep the baby, Carlos more than her. She begs me to call him and tell him not to join the Army and to finish high school and go to college. Then she says her mama is coming, and she hangs up.

"Dang, it wasn't just a dream."

Since Grandma died, I have been having dreams that give me clues or hints about things that are happening in my real life. I am not sure I like the dreams because some stuff I just don't want to know. I should call Carlos right now, but a girl like me has got to get some more sleep. I put the phone back in the cradle and return to the land of Nod.

When I wake up, it's after eleven o'clock. I hear Uncle Doug humming in the kitchen, and I smell eggs and bacon cooking. They must have slept late too. Getting out of the bed, I make it over to my tall dresser and open the second drawer and retrieve clean undergarments. Looking back at my bed, I see twenty-dollar bills scattered all over it. What was on my mind? I grab the bills and decide right then that I am putting most of the money in a bank account.

I open my closet and put the money in the inside pocket of my white down jacket. Today is a shopping day, so I want to dress comfortably. I grab a pink Nike sweat suit and my white Forces and head for the shower.

When I walk past the kitchen, I see the strangest thing. Mama is cooking breakfast, and she has on an apron. I thought for sure Uncle Doug would be alone in the kitchen fixing Mama a breakfast that she would eat in bed. Instead, it's her cooking, and he's sitting at the table grinning. I tell them both, "Good morning," and I head straight to the shower.

After I am showered and dressed, I return to the kitchen in hopes of some breakfast, but what I find is Carlos sitting at the table alone.

He doesn't say, "Good morning." What he says is, "Michelle told me she called you this morning. You and Edith going to the Plaza today, right? I'ma ride the bus up there with y'all. Your mama's not dropping y'all off, is she?"

"No."

"Good, then we can talk on the way up there. Michelle is with her parents at a doctor's office somewhere. My mama is gonna trip. I don't want to be around when everybody finds out. I want to give the news time to settle in, so I'ma go to the Plaza with y'all."

"It will be just you and me. I haven't talked to Edith."

"Cool." He has on his white leather bomber jacket, a pair of jeans, and his Timberland boots and cap.

"Is it cold out?"

The expression on his face is a lot like the one he had when he thought he was going to lose his basketball scholarship to Ohio State. His brown eyes are wet, but he is not crying. His thin lips are tight, and each breath is a quiet sigh. "Yeah, it's nippy."

I hug his shoulders and kiss him on the cheek. "Okay. Let me get my coat and my allowance from my mama. I'll be right back."

I leave him at the table and go back up front to my mama's room. I don't tell him about my plans for Samuel to meet me because all Carlos wants to do is go. He doesn't care where.

I listen at my mama's door before knocking. They are only talking, thank goodness. I tap on the door.

"Come in," my mama directs. She has on her yellow and lime daisy and butterfly-patterned housecoat, and most of the snaps are open, allowing the top of her breasts to show. Uncle Doug is sitting up on the bed with a pillow up to his chest. His cheeks are flushed, and the bed covers are over his lower half. If I weren't thinking about Carlos being a daddy, Uncle Doug would have been a funny sight.

"Hey, Mama, Carlos and I are headed up to the Plaza. Can I get my allowance?"

"Going to catch them King Day sales, huh? That's my smart baby."

Instead of reaching for the cash box on her cherry wood dresser, she looks over at Uncle Doug who nods toward his red slacks. She grabs them off the bedpost, goes into his pocket, and pulls out a bankroll. She peels off eighty dollars and hands me the four twenties. My allowance is usually forty dollars, but I take all the twenties and give her a hug and tell Uncle Doug, "Thanks."

I grab a hold of his sheet-covered foot and shake it on the way out of her bedroom.

In my room, I grab my white down jacket and check the inside pocket for the $300 and add the twenties. I am loaded. Checking my cell phone, I see the bars report it's only half charged. That should be fine.

When I get to the kitchen, Carlos is standing by the door.

"Let's get gone," I say. He laughs a little, and we walk out the back door.

Chapter Seven

"It's colder than nippy out here," I tell him. He wants to walk up to Ninety-fifth Street, which is six blocks up. I agree because he needs to air out his head. It was a good thing I put on my white skullcap. He doesn't say a word as we walk past the brick bungalow houses, some still trimmed in unlit Christmas lights and evergreen wreaths. I don't mind the cold because I'm thinking too.

We are going to the bank across the street from the Plaza before we go into the shopping mall. I'm going to open up an account with $150. The rest will be spent on cheering Carlos up.

While standing at the bus stop, he tells me, "I'm glad she got pregnant. I always wanted to be a father, a real one, you know, like Papa was to us. The question is, am I ready? My thinking is a man should take care of his child, but I am a seventeen-year-old high school senior. My mama takes care of me. I called the Army recruiter this morning, but people have to graduate before they can enlist."

I'm trying my best not to say a word because I am waiting for him to come up with a tentative plan of his own. He always cheers up when he is in thought, especially if the thinking gets him a solution to a problem.

"And, truthfully, I don't want to go to the damn Army. I want to go to Ohio State and play ball, but how can I do that with a child?"

The bus is half a block away and thank goodness because my toes are getting numb. "Here is the bus," I say.

Carlos pays for both our fares because I don't have any singles. There are plenty of empty seats. We sit together in the middle on the side facing the sidewalk. I get the window.

"I didn't sleep at all last night trying figure it all out. This morning I came to the conclusion that ain't no figuring it out because I don't have money or a job. Mama and the Pickenses are going to end up telling us what to do. And that pisses me off because I ain't a man or a daddy if our parents are calling the shots. You know what I mean? It's like Mama will be telling me, my child, and my baby's mama what to do." He has hung his head again.

Softly I say, "You are not a daddy now, but that doesn't mean you won't be. After you finish at Ohio State and get your NBA contract, you will be the best daddy in the world. You will be a rich daddy who can provide whatever your child needs. But you got to go school, Carlos. If you don't then you will be throwing away your dreams. You are a kid, and so is Michelle, and me too for the most part. We are almost young adults, so this is not the time for you to be a daddy. And so what if your mama and Michelle's parents have to raise the child until you ready? Thank the Lord you have parents who can raise it.

"And if you real lucky, you might be jumping the gun. Her period might be tripping because she started having sex. Missing two months don't always mean pregnant. When I started on the pill my period was crazy for at least three months." And that's the truth. I went to the doctor twice thinking I was pregnant.

"She's not on the pill. We were trying this natural Rhythm Method thing she read about."

What smart girl who's having sex is not on the pill? I don't say this to him because this is not the time to speak against Michelle. "Well, whatever, but you could still be jumping the gun." And since he doesn't question whether or not the baby is his, I don't bring it up either. There is no sense adding doubt to his problems.

He looks up at me and, for the first time this morning, I don't see the dull cast of worry in his eyes. The corners of his mouth are slightly up, and the beginnings of a smile can be seen.

"What?" I ask.

"No, she's pregnant. I know it for sure. We do it all the time. We can't sit next to each other without getting excited, and she's just as bad as me," he says fully smiling.

That's funny. His smile and the sun come out at the same time. Either the clouds moved or the bus dove into the sunlight, because suddenly the sun has filled the bus and the sidewalks outside. I like sunny days even if they are cold like this one. It's hard for people to be gloomy with the sun shining.

"Do you love her?" I can tell he thinks he does.

He doesn't answer me right away, which I was expecting. He is actually thinking before he answers. This should be good.

"I didn't think so until last night. After we spent all that time together trying to figure out what to do about her being pregnant. It was like love and concern for her well-being overtook me."

"Oh, so all you and her did last night was try to figure out what to do about her being pregnant?"

"I'm not saying that is *all* we did." He's not only smiling, but I see a little twinkle in his eyes. He's feeling better. "But it was a big part of the evening. I don't want her hurt by all of this. I'll do anything to make her happy and keep her safe. Yeah, I love her."

"Damn, yesterday you were going to dump her because you thought she was bald-headed."

"Yeah, that's how I was acting, but no way. You know I got to keep up my hard guy image around you, but after I found out Michelle was carrying my baby, all my faking stopped."

"Hard guy? Why you feel like you got to have a hard guy image around me?"

"Because you hard, May. I have never seen you trip over a guy. You go through dudes. Walter is crazy about you. He'll do whatever you tell him just to be around you, and you don't give a damn about him. At least you act like you don't, you hard girl."

The bus hits a bump, and both our butts are jarred up from the plastics seats.

"I am not hard. Walter will do anything for any girl who shows him the slightest attention. It's not me Walter loves. He loves sex. Like most boys." Carlos included. He is in lust, not love. Michelle is the first girl to give him some regularly, but if he thinks he is in love who am I to try to change his mind? His current situation requires him to think he is in love. If she is pregnant, I hope he stays with her.

"Why did you do it with Walter anyway? I mean I asked you to go out with him just to be nice. I didn't think you would have sex with him."

"That's why I did it with him. If he told anyone they wouldn't believe him."

"Don't you care anything about him?"

"No. I like him as a person and all, but that's it. He's not fine enough, and he's not cool enough."

"But you gave him your virginity?"

"I had to do it with somebody. I was ready, and Walter was there. I was tired of being a virgin." And I was. "I wanted to experience the act. You'd done it. Every girl at Calumet I talked to had done it. Holy, saved, and sanctified Edith had even done it. I hear my mama doing it and, believe it or not, Walter had done it a couple of times too. After I got the birth control pills, it was time."

"Didn't you think your virginity was something special?" He is looking at me like his shoes are hurting his feet, bad.

"What was special for me was being able to make a clear decision on when I was going to do it. I didn't want it to be a love-crazed act-ion. I wanted to be rational, and I was. It was time, I was ready to move past being a virgin, and I didn't want to wait for love, so I went with safe."

"What about the old guy? Do you care about him?"

"His name is Samuel and, nope, not really. He says he loves me, though, which is how it's supposed to be. The boy should be head over heels for me."

"See, that's why I say you're hard."

"Why does a girl who thinks have to be hard? Why do sex and love have to go together for girls? My mama doesn't love any of the men she dates and nothing horrible has happened to her. She thinks with her head, not her heart. Tell me, is Michelle hard?"

"No, she loves me. She told me that weeks ago."

"So, because I don't love Walter and had sex with him that makes me hard?"

"It's not just Walter, May. No guy has gotten close to you. That's what makes you hard."

"So, Michelle gave you her virginity because she loves you?"

"I would like to think that."

"But you took it without loving her."

"It's different for guys. We got to have sex or else we will go crazy."

"But, you said she likes to do it as much as you. Why does she have to be in love to want to do it? Why does a girl have to be in love to lose her virginity, but it's okay for a guy to lose his just because he's horny? Did you love the girl who you lost your virginity to?"

"No, I was just happy to get some."

"That's my point exactly! And I was happy to get some too, and so was Michelle. Girls like getting some too!"

"But good girls wait for love, May."

"Or, they tell good boys they are in love when they just be happy to get some."

"Michelle loves me."

"I'm not saying she doesn't. What I'm saying is I'm not hard because I made my decision with my head instead of my heart. Are guys in love soft?"

"No."

"Then why am I hard because I am not in love and enjoy sex?"

"Because that's the rules."

"Only for small-minded people. I love you. Should I have had sex with you?"

"That's nasty. Don't say that."

I lean all up against him and whisper in his ear, "Come on, let's go do it because we love each other."

He pushes me against the window. "You crazy, and you are twisting around what is normal and what good people do."

The bus is across the street from the bank. "Oh, we are here."

"No, wait 'til the bus goes around back."

"No, we got to go to the bank first. I need to open an account. Come on."

I press the gray rubber strip between the windows to request a stop. The driver stops right in front of the bank. As we exit from the back door, I say, "They got a motel down the street," and slap him on his butt.

"Stop it!" he yells and runs up the stairs of the bank.

As we sit at the new accounts desk, Carlos's mouth drops open when I pull out my bankroll and hand the white lady with blue hair $160. The lady suggests a savings account, and I agree. She takes the money and leaves us at the desk.

"Dude did give you the money. I forgot all about it with everything else that's going on. May, you better be careful. I'm telling you, men don't give that kind of money without trying to lay claim. He thinks you his."

"He can think what he wants." I decide to really go to the Plaza instead of having Samuel pick us up. I want to spend time alone with Carlos. He needs me.

The blue-haired lady returns with a passbook and forms to fill out for a cash-station card. I say no to the card. My plan is to put money in the bank, not take it out.

Inside the Plaza shopping mall, we are having a ball. Carlos has relaxed, I can tell, because he's talking about badly dressed people, fat people, and ugly people. He's got me laughing, and he's laughing with me. He even goes into the women's undergarment section with me to help me pick out a couple of sets for Mama and myself. He asks me to loan him some money so he can get Michelle a set. I give him the money and tell him to not even think about paying me back.

I buy him a pair of jeans and two cheap sweaters. Things are going good until Ms. Carol calls my cell phone demanding to speak to him. He talks to her, hangs up with her, and says, "It's time to go home and face the music."

An idea came to me while we were buying his jeans. Standing outside waiting for the bus I share it with him: "Why doesn't Michelle go to Ohio State too? She's planning on going to college, right? I hear about girls with babies getting all types of scholarships and stuff to go to school. She won't be the first college freshman with a baby. I bet if you two look into it you will find a way." I truly don't think Michelle is the right girl for him, but he does, and they are going to have a baby, so they should be together.

Carlos looks at me like I am a genius and he hugs me. "That's it. Yeah. She was going to go to school in New Jersey. Why not go to Ohio? With the baby, I bet she can get financial aid wherever she goes. We have been thinking the baby would be the end of everything. Why not go to school with a child? And why not go together? You right, people do it all the time. Now I got a plan to offer Mama and Michelle's parents. A man makes a plan." He squeezes me tighter. "Girl, what would I do without you?"

I don't think the idea is all that, but I accept his accolades. When people are involved in a mess, they can't see clear or past the situation they are in. It takes somebody on the outside of the chaos to see the obvious, and that's what friends are for.

When the bus gets to Damon Avenue, I tell Carlos, "I'm getting off on Ashland. I'm going down to see Mr. Pickens about the job." The idea to go see him just popped in my head, but it's a good idea. I miss the theater.

"Really? Cool. Don't talk to him about me. Did you notice he didn't say anything about me working there? He's pissed at me."

"Well, you are screwing his daughter and he knows it. So, yeah, I think he might be a little pissed with you."

"Yeah, but I got a plan now."

"If she's pregnant." And I hope she's not. "Good luck," I say getting up for Ashland with my bags in tow. When I look back at him, he is looking out of the window, and the worried expression has returned to his face. I get off the bus.

The Ashland bus is crowded, but I get a seat right behind the driver next to a little boy around five or six. He has on a light blue parka, gloves, a hat, and dark blue boots.

"Hey," he says to me.

"Hey," I say back.

"What did you buy? I bet you went to the Plaza."

"I did go to the Plaza. I bought some T-shirts and stuff."

"It's wintertime. Why did you buy T-shirts?"

"To wear under my clothes."

"Oh, yeah, to keep warm. My granny bought me this coat to keep warm. She sent it to me in the mail. She lives in Minnesota with my auntie. I'm catching to bus to Sixty-ninth Street. My daddy is going to be there waiting for me. I can catch the bus by myself because I am big boy, and my mama knows the bus driver, Mr. Jacobs. Do you know him?"

"No, but he looks nice."

"He is, but he is mean to drunk people. He threw a drunk man off the bus last Saturday, and it was cold outside. I felt sorry for the man, but he kept cursing, and there were old people on the bus, so Mr. Jacobs threw him off. You ain't supposed to curse around old people, but I don't curse anyway. Do you curse?"

"Nope."

"Good. My mama took me to the Plaza to get these boots because my others ones got too small. She gave them to my sister. They are yellow so she can wear them. These new ones are blue for boys, so she won't be able to wear these when they get too small. My mama says my feet grow like weeds, but weeds don't grow in the winter. My daddy got black boots, and they are big. I can put my two feet in one of them. Where are your boots?"

"At home in my closet."

"Yo' mama let you wear gym shoes in the winter catching the bus?"

I start laughing. "Well, when you get as old as I am you can pick what you want to wear."

"I'ma still wear my boots in the winter, like my daddy."

"Well, that's because you are a smart big boy."

He grins.

The bus is crossing Eighty-seventh Street. The next stop is mine. "Good-bye, big boy."

"Bye-bye."

When I stand, the bus driver says, "He's a mess, ain't he?"

"He is," I say, getting off the bus, smiling. *Kids can be a blessing,* is my thought.

The park field house is filled with kids. They are running through the halls and in and out of locker rooms. The gym is packed with basketball players and spectators. I follow the wall signs to the theater office. There was no theater office when we used to come up here. Everything happened in the gym.

Inside the office are three girls about my age and Mr. Pickens. He is giving directions to two of the girls.

"Nadine, I want you to work with the picketers today. They don't quite have the concept of protesting for a purpose. They have the shouting down pat, but I want you to explain the passion of protesting. Explain to them that the picketers were there because they wanted change. They were tired of sitting at the back of the bus and being less than. I want these kids to understand why the protesters protested. They have to understand that protesting is more than shouting to be shouting. Create some passion in them. Understand?"

"You want me to get them mad about being Black in the sixties?"

"Yeah, sorta. I want you to tell them what people were mad about in the sixties. Tell them what being treated less than meant. Tell them what sitting at the back of the bus meant. Explain the loss of respect and civil rights. Get them angry."

"Okay, I get it."

"And, Tamika, you are working with the police today. I want you to make those kids understand that police were protecting their way of life. They viewed the black protestors as troublemakers. Threats to how they lived. They were used to black people having no civil rights, accustomed to treating them less then human, and they were angry because the Blacks were trying to force them to change. Understand?"

"I understand, but it wasn't right, and it's hard to show somebody how to act ignorant."

Mr. Pickens laughs. "It's acting, dear, it's what we do. Now both groups are in meeting room one. They are waiting on y'all, so go teach."

The two girls leave, leaving the third girl. I look at the remaining girl and grin. It's Edith. She's grinning too.

"He told me you would be here today."

"Who told you that?"

"Mr. Pickens, when he called me this morning and told me about the job."

Mr. Pickens walks behind his small desk and sits. "Okay, now. I have two good actresses coming back to share their craft. Aren't I the lucky fellow?" He's smiling, big.

"We only get the park space on Monday nights and Saturday afternoons. On Tuesday afternoons we are at the theater. The job requires you to be at all three sessions for two to three hours. Closer to three. The pay is two hundred every two weeks, and I will work you extremely hard. Still interested?"

We both say, "Yes."

"Great! Okay, you are both working one on one as acting coaches with the two stars. You will help them with their lines, delivery technique, and voice pitch. And they are ten-year-olds."

"Ten-year-olds!" we both say.

"Yes, ten-year-olds. Experienced ten-year-olds. One is playing a freedom leader, and the other is playing the part of a state trooper. Both are watching the Langston Hughes play this afternoon, so you won't meet them until Monday."

He hands us each a folder with our names labeled on them and says, "Your tax forms and the play are inside. Your star's lines have been highlighted. Study the whole play and know your star's part by Monday. See ya then." He picks up the phone and starts dialing without a good-bye. We leave.

Outside, walking home, Edith says, "It might be fun."

"Yeah, it will be. But for two hundred twice a month, I don't care if it's not."

"You're right. I could use the money."

"Me too. How are things at Calumet?"

"The same, May. You are not missing a thing."

"And church?"

"Whew, we are doing things there. The pastor gives two services on Sundays now, and ushers have to be at both services."

I drop the folder into one of my bags because I don't like having both of my hands full. Things happen in our neighborhood, especially to people carrying bags with their hands full.

"How do you like the new school?"

"It's cool. So, you know my friend, Samuel?"

"Who?"

We stop because a pit bull has broken away from the man walking him. The man whistles and the pit bull turns and runs back to him.

"The guy you told Carlos about. The one who went to prom with two girls."

"Oh, that dog. I don't know him, but one of the girls he took to a prom goes to my church. She told me about going to a prom with a guy who had another girl with him. I thought the story was funny, so I told Carlos, and he said he thinks it is the same guy you are dating. The guy in the story, his people owned a bus company too. That's why Carlos thinks it is the same guy. So what's up with the guy?"

"I don't know yet, not really, but I like how things are going. He is so smooth." And we both start laughing.

"Just be careful," she says and looks away.

"I will. What's going on with you and dudes?"

"Nothing, and I mean nothing. I want a God-fearing boyfriend, a man who loves the Lord like I do. But, all I am meeting are boys who love sex. When I tell them I am a church girl, they run, and they run fast." She laughs, and I listen. "But, honestly, right now in my life, between church and school and now this new job, boys can wait."

"Wow, you sound sooo mature." We laugh again.

"Stop, May. I'm being serious. I'm waiting on the Lord."

We get to her house, and we stop walking. "Call me after you read the play," she says and walks up the stairs.

"Okay, I will."

It's hard to believe Edith is the same girl. She changed so fast. All we used to talk about were boys. Edith was boy crazy. She was doing it when we were freshmen. Once, she had sex three times in one week with three different boys, and she had no problem telling me about each time. And, now, she is waiting on the Lord for a boyfriend. Wow.

Chapter Eight

As soon as I open the back door and walk into the kitchen, Mama says, "That girl is pregnant. Carol has been over here ten times if she's been over here once looking for Carlos. Worrying me silly. And why doesn't she cut that ponytail? The woman is too old to have hair down to her butt. And she has forgotten that we ain't friends. She's been over here just a-talking, sitting down here with me and Doug drinking coffee with us like she's been doing it for years. Did the boy go home?"

I make it all the way into the kitchen, close the door on the cold wind behind me, and answer, "Yes, Mama, he's there now."

Seeing Uncle Doug still here is a surprise. His party clothes are even brighter in the daytime. He's usually gone after breakfast.

"Good, 'cause I was all out of neighborly conversation."

Mama is still in her housecoat. That is different for her. Once she gets up, she gets dressed. Standing at the table, I decide against sitting down. I want to get back to my room and unpack my stuff and stretch out for a minute.

"How you feeling, May?" Uncle Doug says, smiling, which is always the case with him. I can count the times on one hand when Uncle Doug wasn't smiling. One was last night when Mooky tried to hit Mama. Nope, he wasn't smiling then. Mama told me she likes his smiling. She says he smiles every time she enters the room.

"Everything is good, Uncle Doug."

"Did you find what you was looking for up there at the Plaza?" He takes a sip from the coffee mug. I made the mug for him at summer camp five years ago. It has UNCLE DUG A BUG WITH A HUG carved into it. Since I gave it to him, he hasn't used another cup.

"'Cause if you didn't, me and your mama going out to Ford City in a minute, and you welcome to ride with us."

He must be loaded with cash. He gave me eighty dollars this morning, and now he's taking my mama shopping and offering to take me. If my plan weren't to meet Samuel, I would be going with them. Uncle Doug is generous, and shopping with him is always fun. He likes to laugh and tell silly jokes and riddles that he makes up like, "Why did the chicken cross the road? Because he saw a Popeye's on his side." Sometimes they're funny, but most times I laugh because he laughs.

"Thanks for offering, Uncle Doug, but I did get everything. Mama, I got something for you too. Come back to my room and I'll show you." I walk past them with my bags in tow.

"You ain't got nothin' fo' me?"

Dang, I forgot to get him a little something. "Next time, Uncle Doug. I got you next time."

"All right. I'ma hold you to it."

And he will. He doesn't break a promise, and he fusses to high heaven if Mama or I break one to him. He doesn't care if it's as simple as frying him some chicken wings. If we say we gonna do it, he's expecting it.

When I get to my room, I drop face first to my bed. *Dang, Michelle is pregnant.* Poor Carlos. No matter how positive I tried to sound with him, the truth is his life might be screwed. His mama and mine claim that the biggest mistake they made was getting pregnant in high school. Yeah, they both say we proved to be blessings in the long run, but a person has to get to the long run.

Pulling out the underwear sets, I decide to keep the yellow set, two of the white sets, and definitely this black one. I'm sliding the black one under the bed because Mama will have something to say about the nipple area being cut out of the bra. I barely get it hidden before she enters my room and sits on the bed next to me.

"So, what did you get me?" she asks, resting her head on my shoulder. Her head is covered with a black silk scarf. She smells like the rose water she adds to her bath. Mama likes it when I buy things for her. I hand her the other white set, a pink one, and two deep red ones. She likes red.

"Girl, you must have been in my drawers and seen the sad state of my panties and bras. Oh, I love these red lace sets. They are almost too sexy for me. Almost." She places the sets in her lap and her arm around my shoulder. "So, what do you think about the situation between Carlos and his girlfriend?"

Some Saturday afternoons are like this with us, we two sitting on my bed talking, but it's usually after she helps me clean my room the way she wants it cleaned, and we are both too pooped to pop.

"I was hoping she wouldn't be pregnant. They barely know each other, and now Carlos says he's in love. He was talking about going to the Army."

"Oh, no."

"But he found out he wasn't qualified. Now he's thinking he and she can both go down to Ohio State to school."

"They let kids do that?"

I shrug my shoulders because I don't really know. "I guess so. He is going to check into it."

Mama moves her head from side to side. "Umph, umph. None of this had to be the case. Kids acting grown can only lead to trouble. Don't you let that Samuel rush you into anything, him or Walter. Do you understand me?"

I nod my head yes.

"I'm here for you if you want to talk, or if you have any questions. I might not have all the answers your grandma had, but I got some, so don't play me cheap. I didn't make it this far being a complete fool. I know a little something, but I'm nowhere near as wise your grandma.

"I miss her too, May. Don't think I don't miss her and Papa every day just like you. She was the mama of this house, raising us both. I sure would have loved to see you and her going at it about boys. You think I'm strict with you about them? Baby, bye. Your grandma didn't play. She had one rule about boys: no boys. No calls, no coming by, no going over to their houses.

After I turned seventeen, the rule would have changed to 'sometimes,' but I never made to the sometimes part. I had you when I was fifteen, and once you got here, I thought I was grown. I wasn't, but I wasn't a little girl anymore, either. She did let me date, hoping I would find a husband. I did find husbands, but they had wives attached. Seems like all I met were married men. Of course, I didn't tell your grandma they were married, but who knows what that woman knew? Being my age now and after living some, it's clear that she wasn't too strict. I was just too fast."

I have heard and overheard this confession from Mama before. The first time, she was drunk and talking to Uncle Doug. She told him if she would have listened to her mama she'd have a college degree and be a professional woman working and living on the East Coast instead of living in her mama's house as a single parent with no profession and no education. "My mama knew best," she cried into her drink.

The second time I heard the confession was last year after I got kicked out of Calumet High School. She was putting me on a summer-long punishment, and she told me if she would have only listened to and followed the plan her mama had for her life, things for all of us would have been better. Then she took away my computer privileges and grounded me for the whole summer, which she enforced for only three weeks.

"May, I was so proud when Mr. Pickens started talking about what a good actress you were, but you always make me proud, baby." She hugs me tighter and kisses me on the cheek. "I wish I would have gotten the kind of grades you get in high school. My baby is always on the A- B honor roll."

"Not always, Mama."

"Well, most times. And, watch, when you graduate they are gonna have all types of scholarships for you. And if they don't, don't worry, your grandparents left money for school in trust. And I can't touch it. They taking care of us even from the grave. Her and Papa made sure all our basic needs are covered. Our wants are on us.

"Baby, I want you to go to college, and so did they. Please, don't let a stupid man get in the way of you making a better life for yourself, which is what school will do for you. Men will be here. You will have plenty of time for them once you get something started for yourself.

"I got called up to your school Friday, and your counselor told me you have only been to see her once about colleges despite her many requests. Why, baby?"

Dang, I should have known old nappy-headed, afro-wearing Ms. Stockton was going to call her up there. That woman has been bugging me since I got to the alternative school about filling out college applications, especially after my ACT test scores came back. If I could think of something to ask her or even talk about with her, I would have gone to see her. My ACT scores didn't excite me the way they excited her.

"I don't have a clue as to what I want to be, Mama. The first question Ms. Stockton asks is, 'What do you want to study?' and I don't have an answer. My math scores were high enough to get the attention of a couple of engineering schools but, Mama, I hate math. And, after taking the computer classes, I don't think programming is for me either. I can do it, but I don't like it. If I go to school, I want to do something I like. I like acting, sort of, and one school in New York sent something about their drama program, but Ms. Stockton said that really wasn't a true academic focus, and with my math and science scores I should be looking at more traditional programs. But none of that stuff makes me happy. Acting might make me happy."

It really used to. Pretending to be someone else gave me a break from being me. Not that there's anything at all wrong with being me. It was just cool to be someone else at times. Once I got into character, it would take me hours to get out of character, and that would irritate Carlos to the max because when rehearsal was over, he was back to himself, but I couldn't make the transformation that quick. And since Mr. Pickens told me that my staying in character was a good thing, I didn't try to change it. When I played Travis, the boy in *A Raisin in the Sun,* I stayed in character hours after the performance. It wasn't until I had to pee did I break character.

"So, if we found a school with a good acting program you would go to college?"

"I guess so."

"Okay, then, you and I are going to find one."

"But, if I go, I want an arts school, Mama, where my major will be acting, not a school that merely has a drama program."

"I understand, child. Your mama ain't stupid. Uneducated? Yes. Stupid? No."

I have never thought of Mama as stupid. She has done some dumb, selfish things, but she is not stupid. That's why I don't understand her not going back to high school. If she went back to school and got her diploma, she could get a job and not be bothered with her men friends, but I don't think Mama wants a regular job. She likes her men friends giving her money.

"What about you, Mama?"

"What do you mean, what about me?"

"What about you getting your GED?"

"Girl, I GED every time your Uncle Doug comes by."

"Huh?"

"Get excellent dick."

"Mama!"

"Well, child, you asked."

And this is what she does every time I bring up school and her going back. She laughs it off and stops talking about it despite the promise she made to me when I was a freshman. She swore she would graduate from high school before me.

She stands from my bed with her thin-lipped grin all over her face. "Your Uncle Doug is taking me to Ford City then out to dinner, so you will be here most of the day by yourself. Tonight, Paul is picking me up to spend the night out at the Sybaris, so I have to get rid of Doug before ten. I should be home Sunday afternoon. Paul has an afternoon flight out to Denver. He is picking me up from here, so I'll see you before going out to the Sybaris. Are you sure you don't want to come out to Ford City with us?"

"I'm sure, Mama."

The Sybaris is a romantic getaway spot with fancy hot tubs. It must be expensive because

Paul is the only one of her men who takes her out there. He is the richest of all her male friends. He bought her the white fox jacket I wore yesterday. Uncle Doug paid the down payment on her Mustang, but Paul paid it off.

He seldom comes in the house and hangs out with us like Uncle Doug. Paul pulls up in his blue Cadillac, honks his horn, and Mama leaves. He looks just like Samuel L. Jackson to Carlos and me. Mama says she doesn't see it, but that's who he looks like. Carlos says he's the policy man. I thought that meant he sold insurance until Ms. Carol explained policy as black people's private lottery.

All of my mama's men look different. Uncle Doug is light and kind of chubby, and he was a deacon in a church down South before he moved up here, and he sounds real country sometimes. And there is the flight attendant, Peter, who is dark and thin and always taking her on weekend trips. And then there is Larry, who looks like Harold Washington, the only mayor of Chicago my mama and my grandma loved. Larry is a real estate investor and has a lot property on the west side of the city, according to Mama.

Uncle Doug has been her friend the longest. He came around when Papa and Grandma were still alive. I was a little girl around six or seven

when he and Mama started going out. She's been
going out with Paul for almost three years, and
Larry for over five. She has had other friends,
but none have stayed around as long as Uncle
Doug. He is her first boyfriend I remember.

Sometimes, I wish me and Mama could really
talk. She says we can talk about anything, but we
can't. She will talk to me about her men, but if
I try to talk to her about boys the conversation
always ends with, "You ain't ready for all that
yet," or "Stay a child for as long as you can
because men make you old," or "Get to college
before you worry about all that. There are better
men to pick from at college."

I would like to really talk to her about sex,
boys, and men. Grown men are different from
boys, and I do have questions. If my mama is
aware that I'm having sex, she acts like she
isn't. But, honestly, I don't know what my mama
knows about me. She has never asked if I am
a virgin. I got the birth control pills without
her consent by using one of the fake IDs Carlos
was selling. I went down to the health center by
myself and gave them the identification that said
I was twenty-one and that was that. I got the
pills and did it with Walter.

I think she would have been proud of how I
handled the whole situation since I made the

decision with my head and not my heart. She is always calling women stupid who think and make decisions based on how they feel instead of what's obviously best for them. She says that making decisions with emotions is thinking with your heart. When you decide based on what's best for you, then you are thinking with your head.

If we could talk, really talk, I would ask her why I think more about a man than I do boys. I actually fantasize about being with Samuel. I never daydreamed about having sex with a boy, but I do fantasize about Samuel, and I don't even love him. I just think about him and me doing it, a lot. And I want to ask her why I think about that so much. If we really talked, I could ask her that.

And I would like to ask her, if I have sex as much as I am thinking about having it with Samuel, would my pussycat get stretched out of shape because his ding-a-ling is so big? And, I would ask her, why do boys pop off before the sex really gets started? One popped off while I was helping him put on a condom. I never did it as long as Samuel and me did it yesterday, but I knew doing it with him was going to be different. I just knew it. And, I would like to ask her why is it different, and why I think about having sex with him so much.

"Mama, what's the difference between boys and men?"

"Men have money. Men can afford to take care of themselves and you. Boys you have to help."

"Oh. Is that the same with having sex with them? I mean, do you have to help boys have sex, but men can take care of themselves and the woman?"

She obviously finds my questions funny because she sits back down on the bed and she falls back in laughter. "You know, baby, I never thought about it like that, but you might be on to something." She sits up and hugs me again. "Wait just a little while longer before you get curious about all that. Men and boys are the same for you right now: obstacles that can get in your way. But you are doing the right thing. Study them and watch for the differences. Because the last thing you want is a boy doing a man's job."

She thinks I am only curious about boys and men. The "pussycat stretching" question might give her more information about where I am in my sexuality than I really want her to know. I'll just go online and search for vagina maintenance or something. Some things I need to hide from her. Yes, talking to her without hiding things would be nice, but that's not how it is.

Grandma and me used to talk like that. I had no secrets from her, but I was just a kid. My biggest secret was eating her Ex-Lax for candy. I doubt that I would have told Grandma about doing it with Walter; however, I could have told her what I was thinking about with regard to him. And, who knows? I might not have done it with him or any of the others had she been alive to talk to. But, Mama had me when Grandma was alive, so who knows?

"Mama, Saturday night is a busy store night. Can I open if Walter and Carlos come over?" The store is my allowance money. No store, no allowance. And, even with the money Samuel gave me in the bank, and the new job, I still want my allowance next week.

"Girl, Carol is not going to let Carlos over here after that robbery attempt last night, especially with me not here, and I don't want you and Walter in this house alone. I've been hearing his quiet begging. You might say yes if I'm not here." She says with a wink, "No store tonight. Hey, are you okay being here alone after last night?" She puts her arm back around me. "I can push Paul back to next week if you want me to stay with you."

Oh, no. Samuel is coming over an hour after she walks out that door. "No, Ma. I just wanted the money from opening the store. I'm not scared at all."

"That's my girl." She stands again, this time with her new underwear sets. "Well, I'm going to take a bath and dress up real pretty for your uncle Doug. I might even wear my new bloomers. Thanks again, baby."

She closes my bedroom door behind her. She must be planning on Uncle Doug helping her with the bath.

Us being more like sisters is cool sometimes and, she is right, I do miss my grandma every day. I will go to college if it is an arts school. I need to talk to Ms. Carol about the possibility. She wants me to go to college too. Papa told me years ago that my college was paid for. I guess that's why I never really worried about going, because in the back of my mind I knew I could go if I wanted to. I wonder how many colleges have acting programs. That would be so cool, to go to school and study nothing but acting. No math, no science, no English, just acting. That sounds too good to be real.

I pull out my phone to call Ms. Carol, but I remember she has other things on her mind right now. Today wouldn't be a good day to talk with her about me going to school. I push in Edith's cell number and text her.

Hey.

Hey there, yourself.

I didn't tell my mama about the job.

Why not?

Don't know, just didn't. The school called her up there and told her I have not done any college paperwork. Have you done any?

I haven't done any of it because my mama hasn't filled out her financial part yet. I been bugging her to do it but she hasn't. But what I did do last year was join the career program, and when I graduate I will get a certified nurse's aide certificate, so when I finish school I will be a CNA and I will be able to get a job and get out of her house. A couple of places have been up to the school to interview me already, so girl, God is good. Got to go. I am doing sick and shut-in calls with Elder Wright. Bye.

And she stops texting just like that. No information there. On Monday, I'll go see Ms. Stockton again. She should know something. Maybe I'll go away to school with Carlos and Michelle. Nope. I think they need to be on their own. If I were truly a concerned friend, I would go over there and be part of everything that's going on with him and her and the pregnancy. That's what a real friend would do, but I don't want to hear all the arguing, and I don't want to see Ms. Carol upset and disappointed.

She has been warning Carlos and me for years about the problems of sex. He should have made sure Michelle was taking the pill, but it is the girl who has to carry the baby. She should have protected herself.

I reach under the bed and pull up the black panties set with the nipples cut out. Now, this is sexy. Samuel is going to love seeing me in this. The phone vibrates in my hand. It's Samuel texting me.

How is my woman doing today?

I like him calling me "his woman."

Just fine, now.

What time am I going to see you today, baby?

Maybe in a couple of hours.

Really?

Yep. I was going to call and invite you over as soon as my mother left.

Really, you and I alone again. ☺

He's surprised. He was asking to see me but not expecting to see me, especially not alone.

I went shopping this morning for unmentionables.

That was what my grandma called her undergarments around Papa.

For what, baby?

Panties and stuff.

Okay.

I was thinking about you while shopping. I might wear something special when you come over.

I will be parked around the corner, waiting.

He is a horny boy in a man's body.

Chapter Nine

It took Mama and Uncle Doug another two hours to leave after Mama took her bath. And they were acting so strange when they left that I waited fifteen minutes before calling Samuel and giving him the all clear to come over.

They were behaving like Carlos said he and Michelle act, not being able to keep their hands off of each other. My mama and Uncle Doug were just a-kissing and petting on each other and giggling like sixth graders playing "hide and go get it." It got all kiddie sweet and darling up in here. I thought they were going to cancel shopping and spend the day in Mama's room, but then I remembered Mama was meeting with Paul, and she seldom cancels one friend for another.

I thought Samuel would have gotten tired of waiting and left the neighborhood, but he says he will be here in a second. I wouldn't have waited that long to see anyone. The question now is where to entertain him. If I take him downstairs and Mama comes back, I won't hear her enter until it's too late, and the same with my room.

Matter of fact, there really is no safe place in the house to sneak in company. If Mama comes home, I'm busted plain and simple, so I might as well be comfortable and have him in my room. The chance of Mama coming back in the next two hours is very slim. She will shop for at least two hours, and then they are going to dinner, but things do happen, and they could come back home.

I showered while waiting for Mama and Uncle Doug to leave, and I tried on the new black panty set with the nipples out, but I didn't like how it looked at all. It was too nasty looking. The set made me look like a slut for real. It just looked so unladylike and revealing. A school T-shirt and sweatpants will have to do. Yeah, I was going to give him a little show in the bra and panty set, but it's not in me today. Michelle's pregnancy is on my mind along with what Mama said about Grandma's "no boys" rule.

The door chimes are sounding. Peeping out the front blinds I see his little red car parked right in front of the house. He should have left it parked around the corner and walked over. *Dang, don't he know how to sneak?*

"Hey, baby," I say opening the front door for him. The decision to entertain him in my bedroom leaves my mind immediately. The smile on his face runs it clear out of my head. He is grinning big time and looking like he knows he's about to get his way and that I don't like.

He comes in and hugs me tight and picks me up in his arms. I am about to tell him to put me down but, oh, this is a good kiss. He has a watermelon-wine candy in his mouth, and he is moving his tongue just right and dancing the wine candy from his mouth to mine. And this is the first time I have been swept off my feet and cradled in a man's arms and kissed. And I have to say this is the bomb.

The tips of my ears and my toes are tingling. He must have closed the door with his foot because I hear it slam. When did my eyes close? He's carrying me to the living room couch, and he sits with me in his lap, and the kiss hasn't stopped. I feel his hand go under my T-shirt and his thumb is playing with my nipple following the same circle pattern as his tongue. His hand slides down from my breast to the waistband of my sweatpants, and before I can breathe a protest, he has my sweatpants off, and the same thumb that was circling my nipple is now flipping ever so lightly across my tender tip.

I can barely touch my tender tip myself without squirming, but his light little flicks feel just right. He leaves the watermelon-wine candy in my mouth and takes his tongue to the nipple he was flipping with his thumb, and he spins his tongue around the nipple, and my knees start knocking, and I shudder from the inside out.

"Let's go to your bedroom," he says.

"Okay." *No, no, no, it's not okay.* "No, we can't." I get up out of his lap and off the couch and retrieve my sweatpants from the arm of the couch and slide back into them. "I don't know when my mama is coming back. I think we should just visit."

Samuel does something to me. I get real stupid in his company, and that has to be figured out. He took my pants off, not me. He was in control, and I don't like that, not at all.

"I don't understand. You said you had some underwear to show me. And what am I supposed to do with this?"

He has unbuttoned his black leather trench and unzipped his jeans. In his lap is his hard ding-a-ling, and it's bobbing around with one eye like it's looking for something.

He says, "I got to put it somewhere."

The grown man is acting like a high school boy, but I'm not mad at him. He did just make me feel real good. I sit back down and grab a hold of the protrusion with both hands and stroke my fingers up and down it real light. Then I tighten my left-hand strokes but rub the bulb of it very softly with my right hand. I pump fast with the tightened left hand and continue to softly rub the bulb. I got the technique from a video this girl had when we were freshman. I used it a lot when I was a virgin, and it always works.

I lean toward his lips and lick the remains of the wine candy off of them then I slide my tongue into his mouth and give him back the candy. While my tongue dances in his mouth, he jerks in his seat and a glob sputters out of the bulb and, now, Samuel's knees are knocking. I move my hands before any of the white stuff can drip down on my fingers, but I keep kissing him.

When I stop kissing him says, "That wasn't fair. I been thinking about making love to you since yesterday, and when we finally get together, you use your hands to get me off. That's not right." He's complaining, but he is sitting here with his eyes closed, and a satisfied smile rests on his face.

I ask, "Do you want me to bring you a wet towel?"

I have heard that complaint from boys before. It's not valid. How they get off only seems important after they have gotten off. If I would have stopped rubbing his one-eyed protrusion, and sent him on his way without a release, then his complaint would not have been accompanied by a satisfied smile.

"Please, that's the least you can do since you have me spouting out life juices on your mama's sofa."

Better than in me, is my thought. I go to the bathroom and wet with warm, soapy water the same wash towel Uncle Doug used, and I take it up to him. I do the laundry. No sense in making extra work for myself.

He stands, wipes himself off, and pops it back into his pants. I ask him if he wants a beer.

"Yeah, that would be nice."

Having him just visit is a good idea if I do say so myself. If Ms. Carol or anyone else stops by, they will see him sitting in the front watching television with me. Mama will not like the idea of him being here when she's not, but if we get caught in the living room as opposed to my bedroom or downstairs in the recreation room the chances of her going ballistic are less.

And for some reason, Grandma and her rule about "boys sometimes" after seventeen is strong in my mind. I am still sort of following her rule, and I like that.

I fell asleep on the couch while Samuel gave me what he called a full-body massage. It was his excuse to feel on me, but I liked it anyway. He left about an hour ago. I have been sleeping all afternoon while he's been gone, until I hear Mama and Uncle Doug in the kitchen.

When I walk in on them, they are lip-locked. "Excuse me," I say acting offended.

Mama turns around, but Uncle Doug still has her in a hug. She holds up her left hand and on her ring finger is a huge diamond, and she is crying. "Your Uncle Doug is trying to be your daddy, baby!"

The rock is big, and she and he both are grinning, so I grin and scream, "Yes!" and I am happy. We all three embrace. I can smell the liquor coming from both of them, so I free myself from the group hug. I don't like liquor breath.

"Hey, I thought you were already married," I say to Uncle Doug with the smile still on my face.

"Not anymore," Mama answers. "That's why he was gone so long. He went back to Alabama, found his wife, and divorced her. He wants to be with us, May, if we will have him."

If we will have him. She says this like it's a question, but it's a rhetorical question, one asked merely to be asked, because they both have made up their minds. My answer is meaningless. They are looking at me like grinning idiots waiting for my answer as if it's important.

"Yes, yes, yes, please marry my mama."

I hope when they both sober up this is real because Mama needs to marry him whether she knows it or not. She is so much happier when Uncle Doug is in the house.

"I was trying to get you to go with us so you could see me pop the big question. It means a lot to me that you are happy with all of this, May. I love your mama, and I'ma do right by y'all. I promise to God."

She turns to face him, and they kiss again.

"Get a room," I say in passing.

In my room sitting on the bed, it's apparent that I can't stop smiling, so I must be genuinely happy. This could be big for my mama. *Wait, does this mean my last name changes, too?* I am going to have to check on that because I like being May Diane Joyce.

Mama pushes my bedroom door open and walks in. She sits next to me on the bed. She's not as drunk as she smells.

"He surprised me. You could have knocked me over with one square sheet of toilet paper when he walked in the jewelry store and told me to pick out a wedding ring. That's how he asked me, by telling me to pick out a ring. 'Might as well get hitched. I'm legally divorced now and ain't nobody on God's good earth I'd want to be with more than you. Love you, Gloria.' You know, I try not to show too much emotion in public, but when the other women in the store got all weepy-eyed, I did too. He has always cared about us, and he has always talked about getting a divorce, but I didn't think the man would get serious. I want to ask him to move in, May. And let me tell you why."

She stops talking, grabs both my hands with both of hers and looks me straight in the eye. "If Doug moves in with us, that will make it harder for me to see my other male friends. I am not sure I can stop seeing them as quickly as I should. I want to do right by Doug, and him being here will help me do that. Understand?"

My mama is scared of her own "having her cake and eating it too" ways. But it's a justified fear because what she just suggested has never happened in my life. She has never dated just one man, let alone live with one. This is going to be a challenge for her.

"I understand, Mama, and I think it's a good idea, and I'll try to help too." I hug her tight because I want her to feel that we are in this together. "If you want to be a good wife, like Grandma, I'm going to do my best to help." I hug her tighter.

"Child, sometimes you are wise beyond your years. Let me see your cell phone so I can cancel with Paul." She breaks the embrace.

"All you're going to do is cancel? You are not going to break up with him?"

Mama looks down at her new ring and smiles. "I think canceling for tonight is enough. Let's see how the first week goes with Doug living here."

That doesn't make any sense to me, so I object with, "But if you love Uncle Doug—and I hope you didn't accept his proposal if you don't love him—why not go for it and cut loose from all the others?"

Mama looks up from the ring, exhales heavily, assaulting me further with her liquor breath, and says, "Because child, good decisions are not made with your heart but with your head. Now suppose Doug and me have a major falling out, or suppose for some reason he drops dead, what am I left with? No, child, things are not solid enough between Doug and me to be breaking up with Paul. I am merely going to cancel tonight's date."

Minutes ago, she was wrapped in Uncle Doug's arms, overjoyed with his proposal of marriage. Now, things aren't "solid enough" between them. We all hugged, and I was happy thinking she was in love. But, I should have known better. My mama doesn't deal in love. What was I thinking? It was the huge ring that brought out her joy, not the marriage proposal.

I hand her the phone because I have no argument. "Mama, I'm going over to Carlos's."

What she said makes good sense to my head, but not to my heart. I get my coat from the closet and leave her making a secret call in her own house.

Uncle Doug is struggling through the kitchen door with a green duffel bag and a suitcase. I hold the door for him and grab the top of the duffel. We get both bags and him inside the house. He stumbles to a chair. He is as drunk as he smells. "Thanks. There's more stuff in them bags than I thought."

"See you later, Uncle Doug," I say going down the back steps.

I pull the door closed. Nighttime has come to the city. When I get to the front gate, I see a green Ford Taurus stopping in front of our house. A woman gets out with what looks like a gallon of paint in her hand. She slings the paint over the hood of Mama's car.

"Hey!" I scream.

"Girl, if your name ain't Gloria, and you ain't screwing my husband, Larry, this ain't got a thing to do with you, and if you know the whore tell her the car is just the start. If I hear about her being with my old man again, I'ma burn her damn house down."

If I had a gun, I would shoot this crazy woman right now, but all I have is Papa's pearl-handle straight razor. Mama gave it to me a day after his funeral. I thumb it open in case she comes my way. She gets back into her Taurus and burns rubber pulling off.

"Thank you, Jesus."

I walk to Mama's car, and in the dark, the pink paint has a glow about it. She splattered it all across the hood of Mama's black Mustang. This is going to piss Mama off.

"Damn it!"

It's Mama. I don't even have to turn to see.

"Doug!" she yells.

Carlos is coming down his steps and looking toward the car. He's walking like he just ran extra laps at practice. Something has got his shoulders slumped. He gets to the car before Uncle Doug.

"Who would do that?" he asks.

"You didn't see her crazy self just drive off? It was dude's wife. The one we said looks like Harold Washington, Mama's friend, Larry. His wife did this."

"Man, y'all gonna have to get to a hand car-wash before it dries."

There is no "y'all" in this situation. This is my mama's problem. "Not me. I was on my way over to your house to watch a movie or something."

"I wish that was going on at my house. Mama has been going through school catalogs and Web sites since this afternoon. She is looking to see which schools offer housing for married students. We found out Ohio State won't unless the athletic board approves it. In case the board says no, Mama wants to have a backup plan. Guess what I'm doing Monday after school."

"What?"

"Taking a blood test. Mr. Pickens said it's only right that I know without a doubt that the baby is mine. That made Michelle cry for an hour. Can you imagine her own daddy saying something like that? I said no, but Mama said I had to. The Ohio State recruiter told me and Mama not to worry about a thing. The board usually votes the way the coaching staff wants. I believe him, but Mama is still worried, and she is wearing me out with what-ifs and 'just in cases.' I was coming over to your house to get a break from her. Michelle and her folks left about two hours ago, but Mama is still going strong."

Uncle Doug and Mama have gotten their coats on and made it down the stairs.

"Who did she say she was?" Mama asks.

I look at Mama and dart my eyes toward Uncle Doug, a questioning gesture, but I don't think she can see me in the dark, or she's doesn't care.

"Who was it, May?" she asks again.

"It was Larry's wife," Uncle Doug answers. "I heard her yelling at May when I was going back out to my car. I thought I was going to have to get her, but May opened that razor on her. She's your daughter, Gloria, through and through." He says it like he's bragging, and that makes me smile.

I had no idea that Uncle Doug was behind me when that crazy woman was snapping.

"Come on, Gloria, I got a place in mind that will wash it and buff it out tonight, but we got to go before this paint starts freezing."

Out of nowhere, Mooky appears by the hood of Mama's car, and he says, "I can wash that off for y'all. I can get it all off. I swear to God I can, and I can do it for fifteen dollars."

We are all looking at him, and I think everybody is wondering where he came from.

"Boy, get on away from my car before I hurt you," Mama directs. And, as mysteriously as he appeared, Mooky is gone.

While Mama is getting into the passenger seat of her car I ask, "Mama, me and Carlos are going to go up to the video store and rent some movies, and then come back here and watch them in the recreation room. Is that okay?"

"Yeah, and get me one with Denzel in it, one I haven't seen."

I take a step back allowing her to close the door. I watch the black Mustang with a pink paint–splattered hood pull off.

We were both lucky that Uncle Doug was here tonight: me, because I am certain the crazy woman saw him behind me, and that's probably why she didn't approach me, and Mama is lucky because he knows where to take her damaged car.

"Uncle Doug has been over here a couple of days huh? What's going on with that?"

"Now you know that ain't none of that your business."

Uncle Doug must know about Mama's other men friends. He said Larry's name like it wasn't a big deal. It makes sense that he would know. He's been with Mama a long time. Her ways are not new to him, and at one time he was married. I guess married men have to accept a single woman having friends. After all, they have wives.

I wonder, is that why Mama dates married men, to have the freedom to have more than one man? Well, Uncle Doug living here is going to change all that.

"He's probably going to take it to that hand carwash on Ashland. They're open until twelve o'clock at night," Carlos says. "Hey, did you get the job?"

"Yep, me and Edith."

"Man, Edith too, but not me. And he was over my house, and he still didn't say nothing about me working up there."

I don't think Samuel would go for me having other boyfriends. I think he thinks he is supposed to be the only one. But, should what he thinks be the way it is? It's not like that for Mama. How she thinks is how it is. I bet all her men friends know that they aren't the only ones.

Samuel and I are going to have to talk. He needs to know how it's going to be. He can't have a wife and me, and I just have him.

"May, are you going to just stand there, or are we walking up to the video store?"

"I can just stand here if I want to. You ain't the boss of me."

"What?"

"Never mind, let's go."

Chapter Ten

All our movies came from the two-dollar rental section. I got Mama *Man on Fire,* and Carlos picked out three action movies for us. We are in a "shoot 'em up" movie mood. He puts *Blade II* with Wesley Snipes in the DVD player. We both have seen it before, but watching again is not a problem. He took my favorite spot in the pit, the reclining corner with the footrest.

I let him have the seat because he is still stressed about school and the baby. Larry bought Mama this brown suede pit couch and the big-screen television. His wife would probably have a stroke if she found out about these purchases.

Her having our address will be a problem for Mama. Larry's days are numbered with or without Uncle Doug moving in. Mama is not one for wife drama. None of her men friends have stayed around after a wife stops by.

I want to turn on the recess lights in the ceiling so I can read the labels on the other

DVDs Carlos picked out, but I'm too lazy to get off the couch and turn the switch. It's dim down here with the dark paneling and only two lamps.

Uncle Doug and some of his friends put up the maple wood paneling and laid the burgundy carpet. It's not dark when the ceiling lights are on, but with just lamps like it is now, you need a flashlight to read anything. Mama hardly ever comes down here. She says she is waiting to get a wet bar installed. Once she gets that, she says she will hang out down here.

I am laid out on the long part of the pit with one of the pillows from my bed under my head. I should have microwaved some popcorn, but again I was too lazy to wait for it.

"Do you miss going to Calumet?" I ask Carlos.

"I miss the basketball team and playing on the team. I miss the status of being a team player. I miss being a big shot at school. There is no glamour where we are now, only schoolwork, and I got to do it myself. I am not a celebrity up there, so no girls are volunteering to do my homework. Ah, and you know I miss the babes."

"The babes? Don't you have enough female drama in your life?" I look over at him with my best fed-up look on my face.

"Why you go there? I was remembering good times, and you jump me right back to now." He kicks off his gym shoes and swings his feet up on the cushions. "And Michelle is not a babe. She is the babe," he says.

The babe who has him stressed to the max, but I don't speak to that. Flipping through my phone, I see Samuel has texted me three times.

Thinking about you.

Wish you were here.

Love you.

I am going to call him back. I see one text from Walter.

Where y'all at?

"I'm going to text Walter so he can chill with us."

"Cool. Tell him to bring a pizza or something."

"He ain't got pizza money."

"So? If you tell him to get it, he will come up with it. Just tell him and watch him get one."

I click on his number and decide to call, and he answers halfway through the first ring. "Dang, dude, you should let it ring at least once. What are you doing? Well, come over here. Me and Carlos got some movies. We in the rec room. Nope, Mama ain't opening the store tonight. Hey, Carlos said get a pizza. No, you know better than bringing some beer up in here. Mama will have all our asses. She was drunk when she let you drink that one beer. Get some pop and come on. Bye."

"Told you, if you tell him jump, he'll ask how high."

"Yeah, but I told him you said bring the pizza."

"That don't matter. You asked. That's what's important."

"Is he really as good a thief as people say?"

"Yeah, but he only be stealing out of stores. He is a booster, and his mama a booster too. They got a store in their apartment."

"You've been over his house?"

"Yeah, a couple of times. His mama can cook."

"What does she look like?"

"Like him, except she ain't got those big lips and forehead."

"Well, how does she look like him then?"

"I don't know, she just does. Watch the movie."

"Is their house clean?"

"Yeah. I told you I ate there."

"I wonder why he has never invited me over."

"He probably don't want you to know his mama is a booster. He's kind of embarrassed about that."

"My mama bootlegs and your mama has crap games. Why would what his mama does embarrass him with us?"

"Not us, you. I been over his house and met his mama."

"Does she sell formal dresses?"

"She has all kinds of lady clothes up in there."

"I might get a prom dress from her. Does she sell for half the ticket price?"

"Yep, and she takes orders. You can tell her what store has what you want, and she will go get it, but I thought you and Michelle were going to sew your prom dress."

"Nope, that's what I'm telling Mama, so me and Samuel can have that time together. Speaking of him, I need to call him."

"Why? I saw his little red car in front of the house earlier. Ain't you seen enough of him for one day? Damn. And I don't want hear you talking to an old-ass married man. That shit is disgusting." He grabs the remote and turns up the volume of the television.

"That's okay because I'm going in the laundry room to make the call anyway. It's a very private call."

"I'm sure," he says and snatches my pillow from under my head and hits me with me. I get up from the pit and walk over to the laundry room door and turn the light knob halfway to put some light in the basement.

I close the laundry room door behind me because this is not only going to be a private call but a very important call. This call will inform Samuel that he is not dealing with a starry-eyed little girl who is so infatuated with his looks that she will allow him to do whatever he wants just to be in his company. This call will let him know that he is dealing with a woman who has guidelines that he has to follow if he wants to be part of my life. The main guideline being that, since he is married, it's only right that I have other friends, and I shouldn't have to sneak to do it.

I hop up on the dryer. But wait, what am I going to do if he says no? That I can't see other boys and see him? I don't want him to quit me. I like him too much to lose him. He is fine, and he has money that he doesn't mind giving me. Okay, okay, if he says no then I will tell him that I was only testing him to see how much he cared about me and of course, I don't want to see anybody else. Yeah, that should work.

Sitting on top of the dryer, it's the fifth ring before he answers, and then he whispers, "I can't talk right now. Call me back in the morning."

Click.

"Oh, hell no!" I dial his number right back, but it goes into his voice mail. "What!"

I dial again, voice mail, again voice mail, and again voice mail. He must have cut the phone off. I text: Call me!

Nothing. I text: Now!

I still get no reply.

"Who does he think he is?" I bang my foot against the dryer and jump down. "Bastard." I stomp the concrete floor of the laundry room.

"What's wrong?" Carlos yells from the pit.

"Nothing. My cell phone is not charged."

"Good. You didn't need to talk to his old ass anyway. Come on out here and watch the movie with me. Wesley gonna be slicing vampires up fo' real!"

I exhale fully and breathe in a long breath. *He is married,* I tell myself. "You are being childish," I say to the back of the laundry room door. But, I dial his number back again, and again I get voice mail. The message beeps. I say, "Don't ever call me back. It's over." I am smiling when I click the phone off.

Mama or Uncle Doug must be coming down the stairs with Walter. I clearly hear two people on the stairs. Looking over my shoulder to the stairs, I see Walter's big head and a grinning Edith behind him. I pop up from the pit because it's good to see her. It's like we are hanging out again and I like that. I walk from the pit to her.

Me and Edith hug, and Walter says, "What about me? Do I get a hello, a hug, a thanks for the pizza and pop, something?"

I ignore him. "Girl, what gets you down here?" I ask her.

"My mama was having company, and I really didn't feel like being bothered by them. I looked out the window and saw Walter walking down the street with a pizza, and I knew where he was heading, so here I am."

"Hey, Edith," Carlos greets her without looking up from the TV. "Get on over here with the pizza, man. Been waiting like forever for you."

Walter walks from us to inside the pit. "You trippin' right? You got a five or a ten to put on this pizza? If not, don't say a word to me about waiting." Walter puts the pizza down on the coffee table and strips the paper from it.

Edith and I are still standing behind them outside the pit. "Did you start on the play?" she asks me.

"Nope, it is still in the folder. You?"

"Finished it. It is a very good play. Mr. Pickens wrote it himself, and I think he wrote it so kids could play the parts. The lines are easy." Quietly she asks, "Why didn't Carlos come up there for a job?"

Just as hushed I answer, "Mr. Pickens didn't invite him."

"Why?"

"It's complicated. I'll tell you later. Let's eat before their greedy butts choke themselves trying to eat it all."

The pizza is the bomb: thin crust with big pieces of sausages, lots of cheese, green peppers, onions, and pepperoni. Walter said his mama ordered it for us.

"You be sure to tell her thanks because this is too good," I say biting into a fresh piece. It's a huge pie about thirty-two inches around. I doubt that we will finish it.

"A friend of hers just bought a place on Eighty-seventh Street. It used to be a bakery or something. She turned it into a pizza place. She told Mama she's looking to hire a couple of kids to work there, nine dollars an hour plus we split the tips. We would work from five p.m. to one a.m. on Friday and Saturday nights. She said the tips are anywhere from a hundred and fifty to three hundred dollars a night on the weekends. We can start next weekend, and we get paid in cash on Saturday night."

"What's all this we stuff?" Carlos asks between chewing the pizza and gulping the pop.

"You don't need extra cash?" Walter asks.

"What are the hours again?" Edith asks.

I am not even entertaining the idea, and I don't how Edith could be.

"Yeah, I need cash. I just wasn't planning on giving up every weekend to get it. My mama and her dice games already get two weekends out of every month. So I don't know, bro."

"It's four spots. If you want, Michelle can work there too."

"Oh, you are counting me in as well?" I say.

"Yeah, you can do this and still run the store on weekends. The store don't really get going until after three in the morning anyway."

"Why you so gung-ho on this?" Carlos asks picking up the remote and turning the volume down.

"'Cause it's a job, and I need a job. I'm taking it with or without y'all."

"You said nine dollars an hour plus tips?" Edith asks scooting up on her seat cushion as if she is really interested.

"Yep."

"And you sure Michelle can work there too?" Carlos asks.

"Mama said her friend will probably hire anybody I bring. She needs help, bad. If we go by there Monday after school, she will tell us what's to the job."

I'm trying not to listen and watch the movie *State Property*. I have a new job, the store, and my man is giving me money.

"I could use a hundred plus extra dollars a week," Edith says. "I'll go check it out. What can that hurt?"

"I'll go too, and I'll call Michelle tomorrow and let you know what she thinks," Carlos says.

"Cool, we gonna be running the place, wait and see."

They are all looking at me. I am looking at the television. "Nope. I ain't going. I just got a new job, and I am not about to be working at Mama's store and a pizza place on the same night. I am a high school student. Nope, I am not going. I am not interested." I say all of this with my eyes locked on the television.

"You could go just to support your friends. Go to the interview because we are all going," Edith chirps in her light, cheerful voice.

"You know, I thought I missed hanging out with you, but now I remember how you always took Carlos's side against me," I say, looking at her, and I am laughing because nothing is further from the truth. She and I always double-teamed Carlos.

"What!" both of them yelp.

We do finish the whole pizza, and all four of us fall asleep in the pit. I woke up once because Carlos and Walter were snoring loud enough to make my eyelids vibrate, but I fell right back to sleep. What wakes me up this time is Walter rubbing on my feet, and when I look around, I see Carlos and Edith are gone.

"They just left," Walter says.

"Well, you got to go too. Mama come down and see just you and me here she gonna trip for real."

"She and that Doug dude already been down here, and we were woke, but you didn't wake up. Your mama told us we could watch the end of the movie then wake you up and leave."

I look over at the television. He's watching *Belly*, and it's at the beginning.

"I started it over." He grins.

"Man, you got to go. My mama ain't stupid."

"Are you really going to go see about the job with us?"

"Yeah, I already told you I was."

He lifts my foot up to his mouth and kisses my toe. "Cool. Show me out," he says.

I tell him, "Kiss the other one."

He does.

"Walter, why have you never invited me over to your house?"

"What?"

"Why have you never invited me over to your house? You live three blocks away, and I have never chilled over your place."

"'Cause it's just an apartment. We ain't got space like this. It would be me, you, and my mama sitting up on the couch looking at a thirty-two-inch and not a flat screen. How fly is that?"

"You had Carlos over for dinner."

"He's a dude. That's different."

"Why?"

"'Cause, I don't care what he thinks."

"You care what I think?"

"Yeah, I care a lot about what you think." He kisses my toe again. "See, one day I'm going to ask you to marry me, and all I want in your mind is good and very fly thoughts. I don't ever want you to see me with less or not up to par. See, when I ask you to marry me, you got to think of me as a good provider, somebody you can depend on. That means you can only see me with my best foot forward.

"Think about this. Have you ever asked me for something I haven't been able to give? Don't I always give you more than you expect? If you ask for one pair of Nikes, I get you two. That's how I want it to always be. When I get rich, I'ma come get you, and we gonna make babies and live in a big house with a big backyard. Watch and see. Yeah, I know you don't think it's going to happen, but it is. God told me when I first met you that you was my wife."

"God told you?"

"Yeah, and he told me you don't know it yet, but you will."

"Boy, it's time for you to go."

I pull my feet from his lap and head straight upstairs. I was thinking about letting him suck my breast until he said, "God," which made me think about my grandma. He talked himself out of a little fun.

I'm holding the kitchen door open for him. When he walks by me, he hands me a little black box and stands in front of me while I open it.

"Oh!" It's a pair of diamond earrings, and not tiny chips, either. "Are they real?"

"Yeah, they real. I ain't gonna never give you nothing fake." He walks right past me and doesn't even try to kiss me. "See you later, wifey."

Chapter Eleven

Sunday morning, I wake to Edith talking on her phone in my room. I sit up in my bed and say, "Hey."

She holds up a finger to silence me in my own room. "I can imagine, Elder Wright. Of course, she is upset, and I will have an answer for you before service today. Yes, this morning. I am with his best friend. Yes, I understand, sir, and I will make sure they understand. Discretion is key. Yes, sir. Good-bye, sir."

She sits on the foot of my bed. "Oh wee, you are not going to believe this," she says looking up at me with eyes wide and two-year-old bright.

"What I don't believe is you barging into my room on the phone like you pay rent here and waking me up. What's up with all that?"

Her eyes remain wide and her face excited. "You know Kashia, right?"

"The pom-pom girl at Calumet?"

"Yes. She is Elder Wright's daughter."

"Okay, so?"

"She was pregnant, and she had an abortion. No one knew until her little sister found all the bloody pads wrapped and hidden in the garage. I guess Kashia was scared to throw them away. Anyway, one thing led to another, and she confessed to everything, and she even told who the father was."

"Wow," I say.

But Edith is looking at me hard, like I am not understanding something.

Oh, no.

"No!"

"Yes."

"Not."

"Yes, the one and only, Carlos."

Oh, shit, dang. I stand up from the bed.

"Wait, I haven't gotten to the good part yet, girl. Elder Wright feels that it was unfair for Kashia to have aborted the baby without the father's involvement. He wants to meet with Carlos and his mother today after church service in the pastor's office. The pastor, Elder Wright, his wife, Kashia, Ms. Carol, and Carlos are all to gather and discuss what happened."

Why is she here spreading all this bad news? "What does any of this have to do with me? Why are you here?"

She is smiling a real big smile. "You are Carlos's best friend, and Ms. Carol loves you like a daughter. If anybody can get them to come to Pastor's office, it's you."

"Ha!" I laugh out loud. I look over to my clock. It reads SUNDAY, 7:05. "A person would have to be more than Ms. Carol's daughter to wake her at seven on a Sunday, and you know this, Edith. And, believe me, this is not the best time to go over to their house talking about another baby."

"Another baby?" Now she stands.

Dang.

"What do you mean, May?" She walks toward me.

"Girl, what time did you get up to be dressed for church already? And that is such a pretty purple suit. It matches your coat and hat. I remember when you bought the coat, but when did you get the suit? You know we haven't been shopping together since they transferred me out of Calumet."

Edith holds up her hand like a traffic cop. "May, stop. I don't care about the other baby. Are you going to help me with the Kashia problem or not? This is the Lord's work I am doing this morning."

Her big smile is gone, and her eyes have thinned. She has her serious not playing look on her face, and since it is Sunday, and since it's the Lord's work I say, "Okay, I will call Carlos and see what he says."

The left side of her mouth lifts up a little in a smile. She is getting her way, and she knows it. I pull my phone from the tangled sheets and comforter, and I dial Carlos's number.

He answers on the first ring and sounds wide awake. "What's up, May?"

"You up?"

"Been up for a minute. This girl Kashia keeps calling my phone and hanging up, and when I call her back, she hangs up. Stupid!"

"Not as stupid as you think. She has an issue with you."

"I know, but that was a minute ago, before I got kicked out of Calumet. We used to kick it pretty good and, check this out, she broke up with me, so I don't know why she's tripping now."

"She aborted your baby."

"What?"

"Yeah, her people found out, and they want to talk to you."

"What?"

"Yep. Edith is over right now asking me to get in touch with you because Kashia's folks want to meet with you and Ms. Carol today at their church."

"What? My mama? That just ain't gonna happen, not right now. I could not even fix my mouth to say something like that to her. Nope, nope, and hell nope!"

"You might want to think about that a little more because I think this Elder dude will probably come over to your house with the drama. You better tell your mother before he does."

"Damn, man, she's already trippin.' If I add this to the mix, she will snap for sure. There's got to be another way. What time do they want to meet?"

"After church, probably like one-fifteen. The church is on Sixty-seventh and Halsted. They want to meet in the pastor's office."

Mama and me had gone to church with Edith twice: once to see her get baptized, and on a friends and family day. The pastor was young and kinda cute, but the church smelled like it had flooded, a lot.

"You gonna come on over here and help me with my mama?"

"What? How is that? I can't move your mouth for you."

"You know what I'm saying, May."

And I do. "Okay, give me a half hour." I click the phone off.

"You are going to be blessed for this, May," Edith says with a full smile on her face.

"Oh, you're going to be too. The blessings are just going to be spread all around."

The smile relaxes from her face.

"I feel like a Jehovah's Witness standing on the porch this early in the morning doing the Lord's work," I say while pressing Ms. Carol's doorbell.

"You better be careful, May. That's real close to blasphemy."

"Well, I do feel that way. I just need a church lady hat like yours to match my white coat."

"This is not a church lady hat. Your mother gave me this hat last winter."

"I stand corrected."

We hear, "Boy, have you lost your damn mind? Who do you think you are, Bob Marley? Are you trying to populate the whole South Side? What, do you stick your little prick in a girl every time it gets hard? You are seventeen! Seventeen-year-olds don't get two women pregnant. Answer the damn door before I slap that dumb look off of your face."

When he opens the door, he's smiling. No, grinning.

He whispers, "She's fussing instead of crying."

And I understand. A mother being mad is better than her being hurt. It hurts to hurt your mama. A mad mama is better than a hurt mama.

"Oh, you called your help this morning. You should have called them before you went around sticking your prick in any receptacle."

I think about the girl he did it to on the beach, the one with the stretched-out pussycat, and I think about the bowl of warm oatmeal. I shake my head clearing the thoughts.

Their house does not have a vestibule. When you walk in the front door, you are in the living room. Ms. Carol is sitting on her pink leather couch in her black satin pants pajamas smoking a cigarette with her ponytail hanging across her shoulder and down to her lap.

She exhales smoke and says, "Y'all ain't got nothing better to do with your Sunday mornings than get involved in Carlos's mess." She looks at us, shaking her head no. "I ain't going. The baby's been aborted. What else is there to talk about? May, you go as my proxy. I got enough to worry about with the baby that's coming. That girl and her parents are all I can handle right now." She puts the cigarette out in a white marble ashtray on the gray marble coffee table. "I don't need to meet another pregnant girl's parents. That's it. I ain't going."

She stands and leaves the three of us standing in the living room. "Stupid motherfucker!" she says slamming her bedroom door.

"Okay, I guess we know where Ms. Carol stands."

"Yeah, there is no confusion about that," I say.

"I'm not going either," Carlos says.

"What?" Edith asks.

"Mama's right. It's over."

"But Elder Wright and Pastor are expecting you both."

"Hey, they are more than welcome to come over and talk to my mama if they want to, but I am not about to sit up in a preacher's office and be lectured. Mama knows now. The hard part is over. Besides, what's going on between Kashia and her parents is between them."

"But you got her pregnant," I say.

"No, that's not certain. We fucked. She dumped me. She got pregnant, and had an abortion, and then screamed my name. That girl hasn't called me in over three months. All of a sudden last night and this morning she's blowing up my phone. Whatever is going on with Kashia is between her and her people, not me."

"You serious?" I ask him.

"Dead serious," he says with no hint of play in his voice.

I kind of want to be on Kashia's side a little, her being a girl and all, but Carlos has a point. She has been quiet a long time.

"Okay." Edith flips open her phone and dials. "Hello, Elder Wright. Carlos and his mother have declined the conference. No, sir, they are both quite adamant about not attending. Thank you, sir, and I will tell him."

She clicks off the phone and looks at Carlos and says, "He told me to tell you"—she pauses, takes a breath, and smiles—"he said, 'peace be with you.'"

Edith says the phrase with a snicker. Her snickering makes me laugh. My laughing makes Carlos laugh.

Edith says, "Oh, my God, the last thing he brought this morning was peace, but 'peace be with you.' Are you peaceful, Carlos? He woke me up at five-thirty this morning to bring you peace. Are you peaceful, Carlos?" She sits on the couch, and her hat topples from her head onto the cushion next to her. She extends her legs. "You better be peaceful after we upset your mother and your life this morning. Be peaceful, Carlos!" She is weeping with laughter.

I want to comment, but my laughter won't let me. My best friend sits in a pink leather armchair and sighs with relief. He looks at me and asks, "Are you peaceful, May?"

"No, not at all. Peace is not with me." I sit next to Edith and wipe the tears from my eyes.

Carlos looks over at us and asks, "Hey, y'all, did Bob Marley have a lot of kids or something?"

Chapter Twelve

Back in my bed, under the covers, I am peaceful until my phone vibrates from a text. It is Walter:

Talked to the pizza parlor owner. We are set for the job interview after school tomorrow. Edith, Carlos, and Michele are cool with it.

I don't bother to answer because I need to sleep, but I can't. I have a biology exam on Monday, and I haven't gone over my notes or read the chapter. I have an A going in biology, and I don't want to blow it, and now since the test is on my mind for real, sleeping is out. I throw back the covers and stare at my book bag as if looking at it will make it rise and bring me my notes and textbook.

I get up, hoist up my book bag, and go across the hall to the library. As soon as I sit down at the desk, Walter calls.

"Did you get my text?"

"Yep."

"That's cool ain't it? And Ms. Carol said since it's about a job Carlos can pick us up from school in her old car, so we should all get there on time. Man, we gonna be running that place, wait and see."

"I have to study, Walter."

"Oh, okay, all right. See ya tomorrow."

He is way too happy about working a job that will take his weekends away.

"Okay, chapter eight, cell structure."

The chapter reads straight-forward, and it matches my notes, which is cool. It doesn't take me three hours. I would review a little more, but Michelle is blowing my phone up with texts and calls.

"You know when people ignore a call they are usually busy," I tell her.

"All you're doing is studying for the biology test, and that can wait. I have gotten three calls from people telling me Carlos got some girl at Calumet pregnant, and she aborted his baby. Is that true?"

I tell her, "Ask him."

"I did, and all he said was that it was before he met me, like that makes a difference. I heard she was a pom-pom girl, not even a cheerleader. What do you know about the situation?"

"Very little, but it sounds like it's over."

"What do you mean?"

"The baby was aborted."

"But, she said it was his."

"Carlos was a basketball star at Calumet, Michelle. Girls there claim and have claimed all kinds of stuff about him. You are who he is with now. Don't let their silliness come between you two."

I hear her exhale a deep breath. "Yep, you are right. That's why I called you, May. You see life how it is."

"I am not sure about all that, but I do have to hit these books some more."

"Me too, girl. I have biology the period behind you. See you tomorrow bright and early in the a.m. in lab."

I am so glad my man is not in high school. All this drama is too much for me. I have been ignoring Samuel's texts and calls all morning since he wouldn't take mine last night. I want to talk to him now, but answering his calls or texts is out for a while. Mama and Uncle Doug are in the kitchen cooking. It is time to mooch up a meal.

Garlic and butter fill the air. Uncle Doug is scooping out chicken wings from the fryer, and Mama is adding cheese to the grits, and shiny buttered biscuits are sitting on the stovetop.

"You hungry, baby?" my mama asks.

"Yeah, she hungry. Leaving out of here before the crows and studying all morning. Oh and, May, your friend who drives that li'l red car been by here twice this morning trying to see you. I told him you was studyin', and that we don't visit that early on Sundays. I asked him was he going to church, and he looked down at his feet for the answer. Your mother told him to call you this evenin' after you finished with your schoolwork."

He's looking to see how I will respond to him butting into my business, but garlic fried chicken wings and cheese grits have my attention. "That's cool, Uncle Doug, thanks. I needed to study."

My stomach is tight with brunch, and I am snug as a bug in a rug under these covers, and I have no problem at all falling asleep.

It's Grandma and me sitting on a bus stop bench, and it's summer. The little red car pulls up, but it's not Samuel driving it. Walter is driving the car, and he has a baby seat in the front seat. It's a baby boy with Papa's face. The baby Papa calls Grandma, and I look up and see Papa and Grandma at the end of the block. I look back to the little red car and Walter is smiling at me.

I wake up because I want Samuel to be in the car. I go back to the library and study some more, read Mr. Pickens's play, catch up on my magazines, go to few star gossip sites on the web, search for schools with theater programs, and look up Samuel Talbert. He has a Web site with tons of pictures, and there are other sites that have his image up too. He doesn't text me until after dinner and the ten o'clock news.

Can I see you tomorrow?

If you are driving the late bus. ☺

I laugh to myself.

I figured that, but in addition to seeing you on the bus?

Well, you could pick me up after my job interview and take me to my new job.

Where and what time? I am there!

Monday morning's test went well enough, but my mind has been on two things: meeting the owner of the pizza parlor, and then hooking up with Samuel after. I am not excited about the prospect of employment because I am not working there. It is Walter's constant pestering that has the job thing on my mind.

He's been calling and texting nonstop. And it turns out it was Walter who asked Ms. Carol to use her car, so Carlos could pick him and Edith up from Calumet, and then drive us all over to the pizza parlor.

Michelle is going with us, and that has Carlos all giddy. He hasn't seen her without an adult around since their parents found out she was pregnant, which I don't understand. It's not like she can get double pregnant. The damage is done. They might as well let them go at it like bunnies.

I really don't want to go to the pizza parlor interview. Samuel said whatever I need he would get, and with Uncle Doug living with us my allowance day was moved to Wednesday, his payday, and it went up to sixty dollars. Plus, Mama said I would still get my share from the store. I am going along with all this pizza parlor stuff to meet Samuel, and of course, the plan is to stop by his brother's place before I go up to the park and do some real work. Carlos and Michelle have similar plans. The only people who are really going to see about the job are Walter and Edith.

When Carlos pulls up in front of the pizza place, I see Samuel's little red car three cars ahead. He's standing outside of it. While admiring his stance, his style, and his whole presence, I decide not to do the interview thing.

"I'm not going in." I open the back door of the car to exit.

"May, what are you doing? I told the lady five of us are applying."

Walter looks at me, pleading, but Samuel is looking real good in his shearling coat and cap. So, right now, for me, being with him is more important than applying for a job I don't want.

"Why you going out with him anyway? Don't you think it is a little weird that a grown man with a Porsche is dating a high school girl?"

"Depends on the high school girl," I say and give him a kiss on the cheek.

"May, please tell me those are not the earrings I just gave you."

"Yes, you like?"

"Yeah, I like them. I gave them to you, but I didn't give them to you to wear out with dude. Damn, girl." He opens his door, looks back at me, and shakes his head. He leaves without saying another word. Walter is tripping.

"Are you coming up to the park?" Edith asks.

"Of course, see you there."

Chapter Thirteen

Instead of Samuel's brother's apartment, we are at a motel on Eighty-seventh Street. It's closer to the park, giving us more time to be with each other. He picks me up and gives me a big kiss and tosses me on the bed as soon as the room door closes.

"I missed you so much, babe," he says diving in the bed next to me.

"Yeah, right, you missed me so much that you hung up on me Saturday."

"I had to do that. I was with my wife."

"So, when you are with your wife, we don't talk?"

"That's right." He sits up. "If I tell you I can't talk, I can't talk. And I mean that."

He means that? "What is that like one of your rules or something?" I sit up now.

"There are rules to every relationship, babe," he says while helping me out of my coat. He gets out of the bed and takes his coat and hat off and hangs both our coats on the chrome rack with chrome hangers. He sits back on the bed and starts untying his shoes.

"Rules huh? Well, tell them all to me. I don't want to find them out as we go along."

"Okay, the first and most important rule is that you date only me. Oh, and I bought a black tux to wear to your prom. Figured it would go with whatever color you wore."

"My prom?"

"Yeah, these young dudes be thinking that since they take you to prom they getting some. And that's not happening, and to avoid all that I decided to go with you. No sense in you missing out on an important event like that. So what I'll be a little embarrassed being as old as some of the teachers? At least this way you can still go."

He continues to undress all while he is telling me what I can and can't do. I had been looking forward to seeing him, but after hearing all this, I am wondering why. My brain is telling me to have him take me home. My eyes, however, are looking at his nude body with his eight-pack abdomen and defined arm muscles, and his hard ding-a-ling bobbing up and down. Then my eyes send a message to my pussycat that it's time to get wet, and suddenly I'm thinking about the good time we had over at his brother's house, and I start taking my clothes off too.

Today, I felt like the bra with the nipples out would be okay to wear. Of course, I had to wear a heavy sweater to school and put Band-Aids over my nipples to cover their protrusions throughout the day. And judging by the hungry look on Samuel's face, he thinks my wearing the set is okay too. His eyes haven't moved from my C-cup chest since I took the sweater off. My breasts aren't usually what hold a boy's attention. They stare at my butt and hips. Mama says I have a Parliament/Funkadelic booty. She dug out an album cover to show me what she was talking about. Mine isn't that big, but it's big.

"This is the set I bought for you. You like?" I stand on the bed and turn around for him to get a full view.

"Oh, hell yeah, I like," he answers.

"I thought you would."

"Come here, girl, and bring me what's mine."

The words he said sounded kind of sweet, but the tone in which he spoke stops me cold. He said it like he was commanding a dog to heel. I step down and out of the bed, picking up my clothes, and I walk over to the only other furniture in the room: a table and single chair.

He stretches out across the bed lying on his back. His ding-a-ling is pointing to the ceiling. I really want to get back into the bed, but my brain won't let go of his "come here, girl" statement or his commanding tone.

"You, Samuel Talbert, are a married man. And as a married man, you have a wife." I put my bundle of clothes down on the table.

"Girl, what are you talking about? Get on back over here." He doesn't bother to sit up. He's still lying on his back with his ding-a-ling pointing to the ceiling while talking to me.

"I am a single woman, and under no contract with you either verbal or written. If you think that three hundred dollars you gave me makes you the head of my life you are mistaken. I can return that money to you right now. You or no other man tells me what I can and can't do. That attitude you save for your wife.

"And we might as well get this out in the open now: you are not my only male friend, and you will not be going to prom with me. You are a married man I like, and I have a high school boyfriend, and if I decide to fuck him, I will fuck him. You are not the boss of me. Now, put your clothes on so you can take me to go get your three hundred dollars."

He moves so quick that I didn't see him cross the room. He's in my face with a hand around my neck. "Babe, don't ever talk to me like that." He carries me back to the bed and forces me face down on the motel bed.

"You can keep the damn three hundred dollars. But know this: if we are going to be together, you are only making love to me. No other man can touch you, not if you are mine. And if you ever mention my wife again when we are together, we are finished. We don't talk about me being married when we are together. Understand?"

I nod my head yes.

"And your little high school boyfriend, quit him tomorrow. You over there doing all that big talking but you didn't put on a stitch of clothes." He sticks his hand down the back of my panties into my pussycat. "And your pussy is soggy."

I hear him sucking my juices off his fingers. Oh, I don't know why but I like that. He smacks his lips, and that makes me feel tingly.

"Damn you taste good. You want to make love to me as bad as I want you, so put an end to all these silly, childish games. You my woman and that's all there is to it." He snatches my panties off. "My women fuck only me, so, the question is, is you mine or ain't cha mine?"

I feel his hot ding-a-ling against my thigh.

"If you mine, you get up on your knees so we can go at it doggie style. If you not mine, put on your clothes and hit the door."

He releases me. I turn my face from the bedspread and look back at him. Despite the harshness of his words, he's smiling. He raises one eyebrow and grins wider. I get up on my knees.

Samuel thinks he is in control. He thinks he can steer me around and direct me just like he does to his car, but he's wrong. I got what I wanted plus some. I kept the $300, shivered from the inside out a bunch of times, and he gave me another $200 to get my hair and nails done. Mama cuts and styles my hair, and I do my own nails, so this $200 is going straight to the bank. As long as I get what I want, he can think he is the boss of me.

But, he is obviously serious about me being with only him. I am flattered a little by his possessiveness, but me going out with him alone is not going to happen. What he doesn't know won't get me hurt.

He was a little scary there for a minute. One thing is for sure: he's not like Walter or any of the other boys. I can't just tell him what to do. He knows stuff, and that's kind of sexy. He was inside of my head a little.

"What are you thinking about, babe?"

He's parking his car on the corner of Loomis. I will have to walk across the grass to the field house. It's a quarter to five. I got a couple of minutes before work time. I open up the box of chicken Samuel bought me, and I eat a couple of my leftover fries. "I'm thinking about you mostly," I say. "Wondering do you really love me, or am I just a young girl you playing with?"

He turns the car off and cracks his window a little. "Nope, that's not what you thinking. What you wondering is if our love will last. You feel the love, we both do, so it's not a question of are we in love. The question is will it last. Some love never makes it out of a hotel room; some lasts for years."

I offer him a piece of my chicken, but he waves a refusal, so I close the box. I think he's talking more about physical lust than love. "Are you talking about lust or love?" I ask him.

"I believe lust is the predecessor to love, romantic love anyway."

"So, you saying if we wouldn't have done it, we wouldn't be in love?"

"Yeah, that's why they call it making love. All of the attraction, the physical contact, the kissing, the holding, the copulation, the conversation, are all ingredients that go into making love."

"What about crippled people who can't do it and are in love?"

"Copulation is only one ingredient needed. They are stronger on the other ingredients. Let's say they spend hours talking and holding hands, listening to music, and doing jigsaw puzzles. They're making love, babe. The same with older people. When they are young, copulation is the mainstay of their love, but over time the love recipe changes, more conversation perhaps than copulation."

"So, we strong on the copulation right now I suppose?"

"That and the physical attraction, 'cause Lord knows you fine, and the kissing." He lightly kisses me on the lips. "We got a lot of strong ingredients in our love, babe. But wait and see. It's gonna get greater later."

"Mm, we'll see."

This kiss I initiate.

There are not as many children in the field house as there were Saturday. Mr. Pickens has all the young actors in the gym. He is floating from group to group giving directions and listening to lines. If someone didn't know how Mr. Pickens worked, the gym would look chaotic. But I know. My one-on-one is a thin little boy named Marcus. He has locs and a lazy eye.

"I know my lines already. I told Mr. Pickens I didn't need a coach. You could work with another, slower kid. I'm straight and ready. If the play was today, I would be ready," he challenges.

"Okay, that's great," I tell him. "So how many scenes and acts are in the play?" I put my book bag down on the bottom bench of the bleachers and sit in front of the skinny boy while I pull the folder from my book bag.

"What?" he asks, looking a little confused.

"How many scenes and acts are in the play?"

"Um, I don't know."

"That's okay. Tell me, what is your motivation? What is driving the character?"

"Huh?"

"What makes the character say what he says? What makes him do what he does?"

"His lines."

"But why is he saying them?"

"Because they are in the play."

I smile and exhale. *Ten-year-olds.* "Yep, the lines are in the play. You are right. But an actor needs to know why the lines are in the play. An actor needs to know what the lines are trying to do. Knowing what the lines are trying to do helps you get into character."

"Get into what?"

"Character. You have to become the character, and you can't do that if you don't know what the lines are doing."

"I remembered the lines. That's what Mr. Pickens told me to do."

"Okay, that's a good beginning. Now, it's time to be coached. Here sit here, next to me."

He does, and I open the play.

"This play has three acts: a beginning, act one; a middle, act two; and the end, act three. You see how they are outlined here."

He looks down at the table of contents. "Yeah, I see that."

"And under each act there are scenes. Do you see that?"

"Yeah. Act one has three scenes, act two has three, and act three has two?"

"Very good. Did you notice you have no lines in act three?"

"No. I thought I was in the whole play."

"You die in act two, scene two."

"Oh, yeah, the police shot me. I cry out, 'Freedom,' then fall to the floor."

"That's right. You do know your lines."

"I told you."

"So why did your character yell, 'Freedom,' after he was shot?"

"I don't know."

"Do you think that's important to know?"

"No, not really."

I laugh. "It is, and let me tell you why. You went to see the Langston Hughes play yesterday, right?"

"Yeah."

"What do you know about Langston?"

"He was a poet, and he loved Black people."

"How do you know he loved Black people?"

"Because he wrote about them and the hard times they went through, and he said he loved his people."

"So, you believe Langston Hughes loved Black people. Why?"

"Because he said it."

"You heard Langston Hughes say he loved Black people."

"Yeah, I told you he said it."

"You didn't hear Langston Hughes say he loved Black people."

"I did."

"No, you heard an actor playing the part of Langston saying he loved Black people, and that actor convinced you that Langston Hughes loved Black people because he was in character. He understood how Langston Hughes felt about his people. He understood enough about Langston Hughes to make you feel that Langston loved Black people. He made you feel that you were looking at and listening to Langston Hughes."

He puts his lazy eye and his healthy eye in my eyes. "Oh."

I smile.

"He kind of tricked me."

"No, he got into character. He understood why Langston said what he said."

"Did you coach that actor who played Langston?"

"No, I didn't, but I will coach you."

"Okay, then."

Chapter Fourteen

I'm at the back door, fumbling with my keys, my book bag, and my box of chicken when suddenly someone has their arm under my chin and wrapped around my neck. The chokehold takes my breath away. While attempting to twist myself free, I try to stomp the attacker's foot but whoever it is tosses me back and forth, not allowing me to get my footing or position. The box of chicken and my keys fall.

"Yeah, you and yo' mama thought that was funny keeping my pistols and me getting shot in the leg. Didn't y'all?" He has put a knife to my cheek. Both of us have stopped moving. "Shit ain't funny now, is it?"

It's Mooky. *Lord, how stupid is this boy?* "Dang, Mooky, what you gonna do, stab me in the face?" God, he stinks of wine, musk, and cigarette smoke.

"Naw, I just need my guns back. I don't want to hurt you or yo' mama, but I need my guns, and if I got to hurt you to get them, well, there it is."

He tightens his arm around my neck and presses the point of the blade into my flesh. I'll cut him before I let him scar my face. My hand has gone into my coat pocket and thumbed open Papa's razor. If he doesn't let me go, we are both going to be bloody.

"If you don't take the knife from my face, you are going to hurt me because it's starting to dig into my skin."

"I don't give a fuck." But he moves the knife and lets me go. "Go get my guns, May."

I turn around and slap him hard across the face. He wants to hit me back. I can see it in his face. I pull the open razor from my pocket, and he sees it, but I don't think that's what's stopping him from hitting me back.

"What's wrong with you, Mooky? Dang. We grew up together. Why you tripping like this? Mama was doing you a favor keeping those guns. Don't you know that? You headed for jail or the graveyard with them. What, you gonna go rob somebody tonight?" I lower the razor.

He doesn't answer me right away. He looks down at my feet then up in my eyes. What he has actually done might be kicking in. "What I'm doin' tonight ain't cha business. Just go get my pistols."

I put my hand on his chest and push him hard. He stumbles back a few steps into the shadows of the yard. I can barely see him. He appears and walks from the darkness of the backyard to me stepping into the light.

"What, you now started smoking crack with Blake and lost your mind? You need money to get high? I'll give you twenty dollars. Just leave the guns here."

I would do this because like everybody else on the block, I love his mama. Ms. Holden used to have summer camp in her backyard when we were little kids. We all went down to her yard and played games during the summer: croquet, horseshoes, one-two-three red light, shuffleboard, and she even had a real boomerang from Australia. We drank hundreds of pitchers of Kool-Aid and ate thousands of jelly sandwiches. We had story time and Bible Study. Her camp was the bomb.

"Whatcha care about what I do?"

Looking in his face, I see the sagging bags under his eyes along with cracked, dry lips and old scars on his forehead and cheeks. He's about seven years older than me, but he looks twenty years older.

"I care about your mama like everybody else on the block. I don't want you to hurt her. If you come up dead or get arrested and sent to prison that will hurt her."

He hacks up a ball of spit that splashes against the side of my house. Bastard.

"My mama ain't cha business. Go get my pistols."

I remember when Carlos, Edith, and I thought Mooky was the coolest person alive. He wore Jordans, had a flip cell phone, freestyle rapped at the park, and was invited downtown to Taste of Chicago to perform his raps. He was the man on our block, even if he didn't graduate from high school. He didn't have to graduate. We all knew that other things were going to happen for him. He was bigger than our normal life. Our rules didn't apply to him. We had to go to school; Mooky didn't. He was going to get rich and famous, and we all knew it, and he did too.

"I'll tell you what. I'll buy the guns from you for sixty dollars."

He opens his mouth to say something but doesn't. His shoulders slump, and he puts his knife in his army fatigues coat pocket. "I am tired of begging and hustling around here. I don't need your or anybody else's charity. I will get my own money, and the guns ain't fo' sale. May, go get my guns, or I'm going to drag you into the house with my knife to your neck and make yo' mama give me my pistols."

I take a step back from his threat and hold the razor up in case his dumb butt didn't see it. "I'll slice your ugly face, and my mama will shoot you dead."

If he didn't see the razor before, he sees it now. "So?" he says. "Dead ain't all bad."

"You can only help people who want to be helped," was what Papa said. For Mooky's mama, Ms. Holden, I say, "I'll give you a hundred for the guns."

"I don't want nothing from you but what's mine."

"Fine, hold on."

Inside the house, I walk straight through the kitchen, dining room, and living room to Mama's room. Her door is open, but I don't barge in because she and Uncle Doug are talking.

"Yeah, I'll go with you. I only finished the tenth grade myself. If I get me a high school diploma then I can get into the butcher's apprentice program. I finish that up, Gloria, and I will be making real money, be doing the same job but I'll be licensed, so they got to pay me more. Fo' sho' I'll go back to school with you. And you say the class is at night?"

"Yep, at the library up there on Ninety-fifth and Halsted. The class starts at seven. Gives you time to come home shower and eat, and then we go up there and get this done before May finishes high school. I promised her I would get my high school diploma before her."

And she did. I thought she forgot about that.

I step into the room. "Hey, Mama, Uncle Doug. Mooky is outside asking for his guns. I told him I would give them to him."

Mama asks, "How long you been standing there, May?"

"I just walked up. I didn't hear a thing about you and Uncle Doug going to get your GEDs!" I jump up and down and go over to the bed and hug them both. "I'm so happy for you, Mama."

"You make me sick spoiling my surprises," she says as if she's angry, and tries to push me away.

I hug her tighter. "I'm proud of your decision, Mama."

"Okay, okay, get the boy's guns off the floor of my closet and get out of here. And close my door behind you, and stop eavesdropping around here."

Walking away from her closed door, I hear Uncle Doug say, "I'll probably have to find a new job after I finish the program. Those people hired me because I can do the job of a certified butcher without the certification. They ain't gonna want to pay me the proper rate."

"We will worry about that bridge when we get to it. Let's get the GEDs first."

Standing at the open back door, I see Walter has joined Mooky on the steps. I push the door open without saying a word, making both of them jump up. I hand Mooky his guns. He takes them and limps from our yard without a good-bye or a thank-you. Walter and I both watch him walk into the blackness of the alley.

"May, it hurts too much to be your friend." His voice is barely above a whisper. He sounds strange, far away.

"Did you get the job?"

"Yeah, she hired me and Carlos but not Michelle or Edith. She needs busboys and dish-washers. We will be both."

The light of the kitchen is shining on Walter's face. I can see the salty tracks of tears. He's been crying.

"What happened? Why have you been crying?"

"I lost my best friend in the world."

"Who? Who died?"

"We did."

And he too walks into the dark alley.

After I shower, I warm up my chicken and eat. I collapse across my bed and reach for the phone. I have to call Carlos and tell him about Walter tripping.

He answers on the third ring. "Turn on channel nine, right now!"

I pull the remote from my nightstand and turn on the tiny television on top of the dresser. "Dang." It's Walter in handcuffs. The police are shoving him into the back of a squad car. "What happened?"

"He tried to rob a jewelry store with Mooky's crazy ass. Mooky got shot five times in the chest. He's dead. Thankfully, Walter dropped his gun."

"Will they take him to juvie?"

"Walter is seventeen. I don't know. He tried to rob a store, so maybe he's going to the county."

"Dang."

I call the juvenile court Tuesday morning hoping they have his name, but they don't. Uncle Doug is up with me and dressed in his butcher's apron and khaki pants and a shirt. He is making coffee at the stove. I hang up the phone and wonder if Carlos has Walter's mama's phone number.

"How you like your new school?"

"Oh, it's fine, Uncle Doug. Hey, do you know how to find out if someone is in the county jail?"

"Yep, just go on their Web site and do a prisoner search. Who got locked up?"

"I think Walter."

"Oh, you don't have to wonder about that. Me and your mama saw him on the news last night. He is definitely at the county. A shame, too. I kinda liked the boy. A little funny lookin' but a nice kid." He hasn't looked up once from making his coffee. He dumps teaspoons of instant coffee into a thermos and pours in hot water from a saucepan. "Ya mama said the boy who got killed was one of the ones who tried to rob us. Some people just don't learn."

"Mooky wasn't a bad guy, Uncle Doug. He just got caught up, sorta."

He looks at me now, and he has the typical Uncle Doug smile on his face. "He tried to rob us, May. That's what bad guys do. Time for me to hit the road." He screws the silver thermos closed, puts on a big quilted green coat from the back of the chair, and comes over to me by the phone and hugs my shoulders.

"If it quacks like a duck, and it waddles like a duck, it's a duck, baby. See ya later."

Mama walks into the kitchen as the door closes. Being up this early is not part of her routine. "So, you got a job, huh?" She yawns. "That's good, baby. Mr. Pickens called, and he needs you to bring your social security card with you to work this afternoon. They need to make a copy. I am proud of you. Working there will help with applying for acting schools, I'm sure. Okay, I'm going back to bed."

And she turns and stumbles back to her bedroom.

When I get to computer lab, Michelle is in the bathroom on her knees worshipping the porcelain god. She is emptying everything from her stomach into the toilet. I fight the impulse to ask if she is okay. Obviously, she's not okay.

I pull about ten paper towels from the box and wet them slightly with warm water. I wait for her to rise up from the toilet. When she does, I go to her with the wet towels and wipe around her mouth and neck. Michelle is a mess.

"Every freaking morning for six days in a row now, this is my routine. I am so very tired of this shit."

Wait a minute. This does not sound like the preppy, prim, and proper Michelle I have grown to know.

"It's all just too much. My parents, both of them, are fuckin' annoying, and your friend Carlos calls me every two freaking hours to talk about absolutely fucking nothing. He constantly asks how the baby is doing as if I am some sort of expert. All I know about this damn baby is that it makes me puke every freaking morning, and it's turning my entire world upside down. Things were going good in my life until it showed up.

"I had a cool boyfriend. I got accepted into the school I wanted. My dad was getting rich. I was popular at school. Everything was close to perfect. Then 'baby it' showed up and changed every-fucking-thing. Yesterday, Carlos and I sneaked to a hotel for some alone time. I stripped and got buck-naked. He said, 'No, it might hurt the baby,' and he was serious. All he wanted to do was watch television and talk about going to Ohio State.

"I tried to explain that sex couldn't hurt an embryo, but the dumb jock your friend is kept saying, 'I might knock the baby loose if we do it.' Knock the baby loose? What the fuck does that mean? The best part of our relationship was the sex. He is not a witty conversationalist or an in-depth reader of literature. All the man is good for is fucking. God, he excites every part of my body. Yesterday was our first day alone in an eon, and he wouldn't screw me. Bastard! I hate him and this freaking 'baby it' growing inside of me. I don't want it. Damn, I said it. I don't want it. I don't want this baby!"

She pulls, almost snatches, the rest of the moist paper towels from my hand and she walks to the mirror. I am standing here with my mouth

open. I don't know what to say to her. I don't
know her well enough to comment on whether
she should abort a baby, dang. I look down at my
feet then back up to her looking at herself in the
mirror.

"I don't have to have it. If I'm not ready to be a
mother, no one can make me be one."

Against my better judgment, I ask, "Have you
talked about this with Carlos?"

"Carlos is not being rational. For God's sake,
he was talking about going to the Army instead
of college. Who thinks that? I mean, I knew he
was a jock, but I thought he was smart, intelli-
gent. You know?"

Wait, am I hearing this heifer right?

"Boys. You know what I mean, May? They are
so busy hoping we believe their lies that they
don't see ours. Why on earth would I go to a
state school? Princeton is on the table. I was
accepted at Princeton, and he thinks I am going
to throw that out the window for Ohio State and
a baby. I mean, damn. I like the dick, but let's
not be stupid. Carlos is not going to be a lifelong
thing. After I get rid of 'baby it,' Carlos is gone
next."

I really don't remember when the female
security guard came into the bathroom, or
exactly how Michelle's face got into the vom-

it-filled toilet bowl, or how I ended up sitting on her shoulders with her face in the toilet and her screaming for help. It is all a blur, but I am taking deep, cleansing breaths while the guard and a teacher are helping Michelle from the toilet stall and the bathroom.

We are both sitting across the desk from the principal in her office. Dr. Lee seldom speaks to students unless she is praising them. The Buddha on her desk is holding four silver pens and three yellow pencils.

"I don't know what transpired, but I have two straight A, honor roll seniors before me and neither one wants to tell me what happened." She opens the folder on her desk. "The teacher says he heard a young woman yelling for her life. The security guard said she witnessed one student attempting to drown another in the toilet. However, both students are silent." She looks up from the folder to us. "You two have been in the class all year with no incident." She takes off her black plastic-frame glasses shaking her head in the affirmative. "This will be the one and only incident, and this is not a guess; it is an order. No more trouble from you two. Okay, go home for today. I called both parents. You two report to school tomorrow. Good-bye."

I don't hesitate to stand and leave because I thought for sure I was about to be expelled from school. In the hallway, Michelle is steps behind me. I turn to tell her, "If you don't tell Carlos by five o'clock that you want to abort his child, and that you are going to Princeton, I will. And, bitch, if you ever even breathe in my direction I will beat your ass. I love Carlos like a brother, and if you didn't know that, now you know."

Mama is parked in front of the school, and Mr. Pickens is parked behind her in a big black Mercedes. He waves at me, and I wave back. I hope I still have a job. I get in Mama's car and close the door.

"So, you are jumping on pregnant girls, now?" She is smiling, almost laughing, as she pulls away from the curb. "What happened? Let me guess. It's not Carlos's baby?"

"Well, I don't know if it's his or not, but she doesn't want it either way."

"I knew she did something concerning Carlos. I knew that much. Tell me what happened."

"She's lying to him. She doesn't want the baby, and she doesn't want to go to Ohio State. She was accepted into Princeton, and she doesn't love Carlos. It was only sex for her, and she made him think it was something more. She played him, and she pissed me off."

"Yeah, I think even Clarence Carter could see that. She got you riled up pretty good, but no suspension, your principal said when she called. That was good news. Okay, then, I got two bags of string beans that need picking and snapping for tonight's dinner. I guess that will do for punishment. What time do you have to be at work?"

"At three-thirty."

"Oh, good, you have plenty of time."

Mr. Pickens doesn't fire me, but he has me aside from the actors in the theater talking to me. "You can't get involved in it, May. There is no getting between lovers. Whatever happens between them, let it be their doing, and that's all I have to say about the situation. Get to work."

He stands and leaves, and I go to find Marcus. I find him with Edith and her one-on-one. They are doing voice pitch drills. My phone vibrates in my hip pocket.

I see WTF! from Carlos.

Michelle made her deadline.

"Hey, babe."

I turn and see Samuel.

"We are rehearsing in here directly after you guys." He is smiling, and dang he looks good to me.

I decide to be bad. "Do you have to?"

"To rehearse? Yeah."

There is no way I can sneak off with him. My mama is picking me up, and my one-on-one needs me. But teasing him is fun.

"I do have to rehearse, but I have a private place in here."

"In here?" I'm getting a little tingly. It sounds exciting. "Give me a minute," I say.

I go back to Edith and the ten-year-olds. She is doing vowel drills. I tell Marcus, "Louder."

His voice carries well in the theater, especially for a child. Edith and I smile at each other. Marcus is a natural, which is probably why Mr. Pickens gave him a lead.

I call Marcus from the stage and go over his act one, scene one lines with him. We work until the end of the session.

Kids are leaving the theater, and I ask Edith, "Do you want a ride? My mama is picking me up."

"Oh, yeah, thank you." She's pulling her book bag from beneath one of the theater seats.

"Could you stand at the door and text me when she pulls up?"

Samuel is standing next me. I can feel him without seeing him.

Edith looks at me then him, and shakes her head in the negative but walks from the theater toward the doors.

"Come on," Samuel says.

I follow him through the stage left exit. It's dark back here, but I am right behind him. He reaches back to grab my hand, because he makes a sharp right then goes down the sudden steps. There is a door that he pushes open. There is a light hanging from a wire, and a little cot. A very little cot.

Samuel just unzips his pants and pulls his ding-a-ling out. He tells me, "Pull those down and lie on the cot."

By "those," he means my sweatpants. When I went home early, I changed. His ding-a-ling is bobbing and throbbing. I slide out of my sweats and lie down on the cot. Samuel is not so smooth this time. He is like a high school boy, breathing frantically and rushing. He hardly kisses me and, in true high school boy fashion, he pops off as soon as he gets it in. I am disappointed to say the least.

I am really uncomfortable riding in my mama's car. Not having time to do the necessary clean-up, I can feel some of Samuel's stuff leaking down in my panties. I pray it stops there and doesn't show through my sweatpants. When I get out of the car, I will drop my book bag low across my hips and butt.

"So, Edith, how is school, and how is your mother?"

"School is fine. I will graduate with a CNA certificate. My mama is okay."

"Are you going to nursing school?"

"No, ma'am, not right now. I just want a job so I can move out on my own. Maybe later, I will work for a company that will pay my tuition."

"What's the rush to move out?"

"I need a better, a more Christian environment than my mother's home. We are not spiritually yoked."

"Oh, I see." And my mama says nothing else until she drops Edith off.

"Good-bye, baby. Give your mother my best."

"I will, ma'am. Thank you for the ride."

Edith doesn't tell me to call her later, and she didn't say one word to me on the ride home. I will worry about her later. Right now, I need the bathroom.

Cleaned up and relaxing across my bed, I see Carlos has called me seven times, and I have three texts from him. I call him back.

"She broke up with me."

I want to ask, "Who?" so bad, but I don't. "Did she say why?"

"Because she doesn't love me, and she wants to abort the baby."

"And how do you feel?"

"All messed up, because I am relieved and hurt. I couldn't suggest an abortion to her because she was always talking about how much she loved me. But now she's saying she never really loved me, and she's going to Princeton."

"Did she ask you for any money for the abortion?"

"No. Her mother called and asked to speak to my mother, and they talked it out."

"You still love her?"

"May, I don't know how I feel."

Wednesday morning, I am the only girl in computer lab, no Michelle. At lunch, Samuel sends me pictures of his ding-a-ling. I get kind of tingly looking at them. I wonder if he sends his wife these kinds of pictures and if she gets tingly looking at them.

Samuel sends me a text: No more quickies.

What is a quickie?

Fast sex.

Oh, okay.

He sends video of his ding-a-ling. He is jacking off, and I watch as he goes to climax. He squirts all over himself, dang. I wish I was there. I am feeling way past tingly. I need to see my man.

I keep looking at the ding-a-ling pictures all through my next class. I make myself put the phone in my locker.

After dinner, Samuel sends me a text, asking: Can you get out?

How the hell does he think I can get out?

No.

Why?

Because it's a school night.

I am taking your bus route tomorrow, fuck rehearsal.

Okay.

He sends another jacking-off video. I go to sleep watching the videos.

Thursday morning, still no Michelle in computer lab. If she were my friend, I would be worried. Between classes, I go Carlos's locker. He is stuffing in his book bag.

"Hey, any news on Michelle?"

"Yep. She transferred to Princeton's prep school in New Jersey."

"What?"

"Yep, her mom told my mama last night. They are driving her up there right now."

I lower my voice and ask, "What about the abortion?"

"I guess she had it. My mama thinks it's done."

"Dang, I don't think a long car ride would be recommended after that type of procedure."

"I don't know and I don't care, May. You know I took the pizza parlor job, right? And she be working the hell out of me every day after school. It is just her husband, her, her son, and me. I didn't tell them Walter went to jail, but they never asked about him, so I guess they know. But, I am making a ton of money. Last night I made sixty dollars."

"Really?"

"Really. The place is crowded every night. You should come on down."

"No, I'm good. Wow, Michelle just left, huh?"

"Yep, and the baby is gone."

Thursday after school, Samuel is the bus driver, and he did what my mama warned him against. He veered off the bus route to his brother's apartment.

It is just me and him like before, and he kisses me like before, and he holds me like before, but it isn't like before. I barely shiver from the inside out. He seems just as satisfied though, but I'm not.

"Are you okay, babe?" he asks with his head on the pillow with me.

I look at him, and I am not thrilled.

His phone rings, and he jumps out of bed to take the call. I dress while he talks. I can hear a woman's voice. And he's lying about where he is. I am guessing it is his wife.

On Friday, he doesn't call me and I don't call him. I delete all the pictures and videos of his ding-a-ling from my phone.

Chapter Fifteen

Saturday, at Mooky's funeral, everybody is sad not for him, but for his mama. None of the people in attendance have really viewed his body. Everyone walks up the middle aisle, quickly peeps into the gray casket at Mooky in his purple suit lying on sky blue pillows, and then they proceed to Ms. Holden.

She said that the purple suit was his favorite, but it is still a painful fashion sight on those sky blue pillows. If I were sitting next to Edith or Carlos, that color catastrophe would be discussed, at a funeral or not. Sitting next to Ms. Holden, I notice that people are here to pay their respects to the mama, not the dead son, and I think that's sad.

Every life deserves some type of recognition when it's over. The least folks could do is stop at his casket. I don't think a quick pass by is right. Mooky lived a life, and his life was worth a pause at his remains.

The saxophone is the only instrument playing, and the choir is softly humming. I recognize the melody, but the name of the song will not come to mind. Ms. Holden is humming the melody with the choir. The saxophone player stands, walks past the drummer, and faces us in the front row. The notes are soothing. I hope Ms. Holden finds comfort in the music.

Last night she called Carlos, Edith, and me and requested that the three of us ride in the family limo with her. "The only real family I had up here was that boy, and now he's gone. I need you kids tomorrow. I need y'all close to me." We all agreed. How could we not?

This is the third time I have sat in the front row at Miles Temple CME Church, and neither time has it felt like an honor. I remember Grandma telling me the front row was for church leaders and visiting dignitaries. The only dignitary in the row today is Ms. Holden. She is special to everybody in the neighborhood. She has closed her eyes and is slowing rocking to the music of the saxophone player. He is soothing her.

Papa used to say, "That Ms. Holden will give anybody in need the shirt off her back," and he wasn't exaggerating. Ms. Holden is known to give people the food off of her stove. I have seen her taking breakfast and dinner to sick people on the block. She is always helping older people get to the store, and she goes over to help young mothers when they come home from the hospital.

While Mama was doing my hair this morning, she told me that Ms. Holden was a midwife down South, but once she came up here, she got a job as an inspector with the city's health department and retired from that. Ms. Holden and my grandma were friends. She has been over a couple times since my grandparents died, usually around Thanksgiving and Christmas. Mama is respectful toward her but not friendly. She calls her "an old busybody" and says she's nosey, but when Mama had walking pneumonia, it was Ms. Holden who came down the block with teas, herbs, moldy bread, oranges, and garlic that got her better.

I don't think either Mama or me has been in Miles Temple since my grandma's funeral. This was her church, and we went with her. She sat five pews back on the corner. I can't recall her missing a Sunday. I truly feel sad for Ms. Holden's loss, but I am happy to be in Grandma's church again. Maybe I'll start attending service once in a while. I haven't worn my Sunday dresses in a long time.

Dressing up for church was fun. Mama, Grandma, and me would get really sharp. Grandma would remind me that going to church wasn't about the dressing up: "We are going to praise Him and let Him know we love Him, and to be dutiful in this Christian life." I went to dress up, and I think Mama went for the same reason as me. Papa would whistle at us as we left him sitting on the back steps or at the kitchen table with his coffee and toasted onion roll.

Today, Edith is the one who is sharp. I have to hand it to her. She looks regal in her black dress, pearls, stockings, and heels, but she always wears the right thing at the right time. I have on a black dress but no pearls, and I am wearing flats. My hair is curled with a hanging twist, but Edith's short-cut waves with longer curls on the top is classier. She looks grown.

Carlos has on a black suit with a white shirt and a yellow tie. Ms. Carol must have matched up the outfit for him because Carlos would not have worn a tie. She's clean too, sitting behind us in a two-piece black suit with a lace charcoal gray blouse.

Sitting next to Ms. Holden, I can tell she is overtaken by her grief, and she is hurting. She hasn't stopped wiping away tears since we sat down. I have been holding her hand and nodding my head with her. The only thing I can think to say is, "He loved you, Ms. Holden. He really did."

"I know, child," is her answer, but her eyes remain tearful despite the saxophone player's soothing. I guess nothing short of Mooky getting up out of that casket would really ease her pain.

"You kids got to get out of this city, go away to school, get your degrees, and then come back if you want. Staying here ain't good for y'all. The streets will pull you down. Y'all promise me y'all gonna go away to school. Promise me right now."

She is looking down the pew at each of us. I see that her mascara has run and made dark lines on her fudge-colored cheeks. The crying and tears have turned her eyes into peppermint, and the pink stripes are taking over the white. I want to tell her to wipe her nose, but I don't want to embarrass her.

We are all high-school seniors, and I think the only person who has concrete plans of going away to school is Carlos, but we each answer, "Yes, ma'am, I am going away. I promise."

She looks each of us in the face and says, "I'm holding you to it. Carlos, Edith, and May, each of you have sat in the house of God and made a promise to go away to school. And y'all better keep it, and get out of this neighborhood before the streets do to you what they did to my Mooky.

Don't think it can't happen to y'all, because it can. He wasn't the best boy, but he wasn't the worst. A little bad turned a lot bad out there on those streets. He wasn't an angel. Lord, I know that, but he was mine. Mine. My baby is gone. Mine. My baby boy, my only child, is gone."

She's talking loud now, almost screaming, and I don't know what to do to calm her down.

"Why, Lord, why? He woulda changed, he really woulda changed, Lord. He was tryin', Lord. You coulda given him mo' time, Lord. You coulda!"

She is no longer looking at us or holding my hand. She is hugging herself and rocking back and forth. The saxophone gets louder. Ms. Carol comes to her and wraps her arms around her. I move down the pew allowing her to sit next to Ms. Holden. Looking at both of them, I can tell Ms. Carol's hug is one of restraint more than comfort. Ms. Holden wants to stand and scream out.

"His daddy died the same way, Lord. Shot down by the police. You coulda spared the son, Lord. You coulda spared my son, Lord!"

Ms. Holden breaks free of Ms. Carol's hugs and reaches her arms to the heavens. She hangs her head and wails a sorrowful moan that rips through me, and, now, I am crying.

I'm thinking about the big boy Mooky: the one who buried my dead hamster in the backyard and had church service for her; the one who taught Carlos how to ride a bike; the one who beat up the boy who popped my training bra strap at the park. Mooky was the big boy on the block who looked out for us little kids.

That Mooky is dead too. I had forgotten that Mooky until his mama's cry shook him loose in my mind. Mooky was more to me than the addict thug he had become. I stand with his mama and cry.

The melody is from the song "Jesus Be a Fence Around Me." The choir is singing it now. I walk to the casket and look at Mooky. I see the boy he was. I see his mama's son. And, yes, he will be missed. I too start to sing the song: "'This is my prayer I pray each and every day. That you will guide my footsteps lest I stumble and stray.'"

The church is vibrating with the chorus. The choir and the people in the pews are loudly singing the song. "Yes, Lord!" reverberates off the walls and ceiling.

Suddenly I feel off-balance, not centered. I move away from the casket before I topple it over. I want to sit down, but I don't think I can take a sure step backward or forward. A coldness is around me. I wrap my arms around myself from the chill. My teeth are chattering.

"Yes, Lord!" I sing with everyone else in the church.

I turn around to look for my mama, and I spot her and Uncle Doug about eight pews back, but in the fifth row, sitting on the corner, it looks like . . .

"'Jesus, I want you to protect me as I travel along the way.'" The choir, the people, and I sound like one voice.

"'Yes, Lord, I know you can, yes, Lord,'" the one voice of the church screams.

I blink my eyes closed and hold them closed. Who I thought I saw couldn't be.

When I open them, she's still there nodding her head to the time of the music. She is wearing her yellow and gold Sunday hat with her Saint's Day white dress on. She smiles at me.

"Yes, Lord!" shakes the pews. The drums, the drums, the one voice and the drums are all I hear.

When I look again to my mama, she's looking at her too. My mama stands and stretches her arm high. "Yes, Lord!" she screams within the one voice.

I feel light in the head and feet. I feel my feet stomping the floor. The voice of the church and the beat of the drums are moving all through me.

"Yes, Lord!" is my scream. My feet are moving, but not by my command. None of these steps I know.

My grandma is beside me. My mama comes down to us, and we three are together. My mama is holding me tight, but my arms are raised high.

"Don't leave us!" Mama screams but Grandma rises above us, above the choir, and her arms reach to Ms. Holden, who doesn't seem to see her, and then she's gone. I can barely breathe, and I've gone from cold to hot. I am so hot now that sweat has drenched me. My feet are still dancing.

Mama is dancing with me. Her hands are on my shoulders and mine are on hers, our feet stomping to the beat of the drums. Every bang, every boom, is a step. I look up, and I see wooden rafters are bending. I want to float high. I want to go with Grandma. I'm jumping now, jumping as high as I can but I can't stay up. I can't fly. The floor becomes the ceiling, and I am rolling on it to my mama's feet. I grab her legs and cry out for my grandma.

I come to in the pastor's office. Carlos and I were brought here when we were kids because both of us had taken money out of the collection plates on Youth Day. We were passing the plates among the congregation, and when the time came to dump the plates into the larger basket, he kept a little, and I kept a little. The funny part was he was on one side of the church and I was on the other. We didn't influence each other, but we committed the same act. The grownups didn't find the act funny. We were both spanked right here in the pastor's office by Grandma.

"May, you were Holy Ghost filled!"

It's Edith fanning me. I am stretched on the pastor's marshmallow white leather couch.

"The whole church was in the spirit. Even your mama got happy. People who have never felt the spirit got filled today. Reverend is still bringing in new sheep to his flock. Six people joined. That has never happened at a funeral I went to before."

I sit up a little and brush at my skirt. "The funeral is still going on? How long have I been in here?"

A heavy throat clearing is heard. "I don't know if you will call it a funeral anymore. It's church going on down there." It's a man's voice.

I sit all the way up, and standing in the doorway is the saxophone player.

"I am glad to see you are okay. I was worried about you, gorgeous. Seldom do I play churches, so you kind of shocked me passing out like that from the music."

Edith blows a long breath and smacks her gloss-covered lips. She stops fanning me and turns her attention to the saxophone player in the doorway. "It wasn't the music. It was the Holy Ghost. The music called the Spirit, and once He came people got happy," Edith answers as if she is talking to an ignorant heathen.

"Okay," he agrees with a shrug of his broad shoulders. To me, he says, "But how are you doing, gorgeous?"

He says "gorgeous" like it's my name and I am titillated by the sound of it. He has a gray and black ponytail that hangs over his left shoulder, and the end is tied with blue beads. He has light brown walnut-colored eyes and a long, narrow nose and thin lips. If not for his skin matching his eyes, his face would look like a white man's. He has what Mama calls European features.

"My name is May. May Diane Joyce."

"Please to meet you, May. But you are gorgeous. The finest woman I seen in seven years."

Why would a man with European features find my full lips and broad nose gorgeous? Mama says Mississippi is all over my face despite my complexion.

"May ain't a woman. She's seventeen and still in high school. You better leave. This is a church."

He adjusts the shoulder strap of the black case on his shoulder and says, "I am leaving. I just stopped by to check on her." He steps into the office and hands me his card. "Give me a call this evening. I would like to invite you to a show at my club."

"Your club?" I ask.

"Yeah, I own the Jazzy Blues."

"On Halsted? My mama goes to that club."

"Good, bring her too. I would love to see the woman who created such beauty. See you tonight," he says with a nod. He turns and leaves.

"That man was trying to get with you in a church," Edith says sitting next to me on the couch. She is looking at his card with interest and touches it. "It's printed on silk or something. 'Nelson Brown, Proprietor.' Do you think he really owns it? Anita Baker sang there. So did Sade, and Patti Austin. All the jazz singers go to that club."

"How do you know?"

"I love jazz."

"You want to go with me if Mama takes me?"

"Girl, I do. But, that man tried to get with you in church. He's got the devil in him. I can't go."

"Correction: he did get with me in church, and, girl, did you see that he was bowlegged?"

"No. I saw that he is old as black pepper, and he was wearing a wedding band. That's what I saw."

"He's not that old. I doubt that he's forty, but he sure can play that saxophone. I read that musicians and artists are sensual lovers because they are so in touch with their creative selves."

"May! He had on a wedding ring, and you are in church. You were just filled with the Holy Spirit." She puts her hands together in prayer and says, "Lord, she don't know what she's saying. Please don't smite her."

I can't tell if she is joking or serious. She keeps her hands joined in prayer and mumbles something I can't make out. Would the Lord smite me for what I said? Could He? And what exactly is smiting? Something did just have me dancing around like a chicken and hallucinating. It's time to go. I need to ask Mama if I saw what I thought I saw, and I need to ask her about going to the nightclub because I definitely want to go.

"See, that's why you should go to the nightclub, to stop me from doing something that will get me in trouble with the Lord."

She stops praying, and her eyes are back on the card. It's apparent that Edith wants to go to the club. She just needs a reason.

"I heard on the radio that Wynton Marsalis has been playing there all week. Hearing him play would be something," she says.

"I'll have my mama call your mama."

"My mama is too busy to care what I do. You know what? Come on by and get me if you all go. I do want to go, and I will be doing my Christian duty by keeping you away from that sinful man."

"Good. Let's get out of here and go find my mama." I stand with her assistance.

"May?" It's Uncle Doug in the doorway. "Your mama is in the car. Are you ready, darlin'?"

"Yep, I'm all better."

Chapter Sixteen

Mama is playing asleep in the front seat of Uncle Doug's black Buick Roadmaster. She does this when she doesn't want to talk about something, but we're talking about this.

"Did you see her, Mama?"

She moans a phony sleepy response.

"Mama!" I say louder to the back of her head.

"What?" she snaps back.

"Did you see her?"

"See who?"

"Don't play with me, Mama. You saw her didn't you?"

She breathes a long breath, says nothing, and still nothing. "We will talk about it at home, you and me."

And I can tell she is finished with it for now.

"Mama, you and Uncle Doug and me and Edith got invited to a jazz show tonight. And guess where it's at?"

"Who invited us to a show?"

"The owner of the club, a man named Nelson Brown."

"Yeah, I saw him eyeing you while he was supposed to be playing for the Lord. That man has been a dog all his life. And married to a good woman, an accountant. They been together for years, got kids and grandkids, but he still sniffing around young girls. So, he's trying to hit on my baby huh? I bet he called you 'gorgeous' and said you was the most beautiful woman he'd seen in ten years. Didn't he?"

Now how does she know that? "He said seven years."

Both of them start laughing in the front seat.

"You know what, baby? We going. I would pay good money to see his face when he finds out I'm your mama."

I have to ask her this question: "Did you and him go out?"

"Oh, hell no. That horn-playing man is too cheap, and he thinks he's fine. The bowlegged joker thinks women are supposed to do for him." She turns in her seat to face me. "But he is a very rich man, May. Much wealthier than your little bus driver friend. He has recorded albums, and he has another jazz club in Los Angeles. He drives a Bentley and lives downtown, a block away from the mayor."

Uncle Doug grunts, "Money ain't everything, Gloria." He turns the corner deep and shifts us in our seats to the right. "That man is only ten years or so younger than me, and he married." He exhales a grunt.

Mama turns back around and faces him. "There is a big difference in their ages, that's true. Let me see, you're what, twenty-three years older than me?" She places her hand on his thigh. "And, if I'm not mistaken, when you met me you had a wife, and you kept her for a number of years after you knew me, and we turned out just fine. Now, didn't we?"

Dang, she put him on the spot with that one, but Uncle Doug knows getting into my mama's business is risky. He blows a breath and rolls his window down a little, letting in the brisk afternoon air.

"Yeah, that's true. We turnin' out pretty good, but you didn't have me for an uncle. If I woulda been around, I woulda run a man old as me away from you, run him clean off of the block."

Mama smiles big, showing most of her teeth. "Well, it's a good thing you wasn't around because I like how we turned out." She leans over and kisses him on the cheek.

"But him and her ain't me and you, sugar. Times is different now. He is too old for her. We were the end of a time. Young women nowadays ain't got to be bothered with no old buzzards helpin' them to get by. Most of them makin' more money than men anyway, gettin' they college degrees and everythin'. How we lived ain't how she got to leave. She smart. She gonna go to college." He is talking to Mama, but he is looking at me in the rearview mirror, smiling and nodding his head.

"Relax about this, Douglas. I know what's best for my child."

He groans gruffly and moans. "You ain't hearin' me on this, woman. You always want things to go yo' way but, like they say, it takes a village to raise a child. You got to listen to other people sometimes. And I'm right about this. He too old for her. We should be runnin' that man away from her, not encouragin' them to be together."

Mama's thin lips have tightened, and all playfulness is gone from her face. "Are you telling me how to raise my daughter, one who is already raised? And I hope you don't think you know what's best for my child."

"Gloria, I got an opinion, and it's my duty as a man to say somethin' about a child bein' raised wrong. And she ain't grown yet."

"She's the same age I was when you met me."

"But you had a child, and you was way more womanly than that girl."

"Womanly?"

"Womanly, worldly, whatever, you was mo' grown up than May is now. You know that."

The play has returned to Mama's face. "What are you saying, Doug? That I worked my womanly ways on you?"

"Stop that now. We talkin' serious, and you ain't gonna get me off the subject."

"Oh, stop all that fussing, Doug, and come on over here. This worldly woman has got something for you."

Mama tries to move in for another kiss, but he hits the brakes hard, almost making Mama and me pop up off our seats.

"Damn, that pigeon almost flew right into the windshield," he says.

Mama and I are both looking out the windows for a bird. There is none in sight.

"Pigeon my ass," is my mama's reply.

Uncle Doug starts laughing.

When I get home, I go straight to my room and reach under the bed. That's where Mama keeps Grandma's quilts and comforters. I pull out the big clear plastic square with the biggest quilt in it. I unzip the square and yank the quilt from it. This was the last one she made. I wrap myself in it and fall across the bed. I am asleep before I can kick off my other shoe.

We are back at the church, Mama, Grandma, and me. We three are sitting alone on the front pew looking at the empty pulpit.

"He won't be with you long," is said but none of us is speaking,

"Enjoy this time, daughter. He has a good heart. Don't let the lost tear you down. God's will will be done. Hard times are ahead for you and the child. I have stayed with you both past my time, trying to make sure you could stand, but you are past being a sapling. You have to weather the winds of life. Your roots are deep, and all storms pass.

"This place, this church, is your home as much as it is mine. Bring the child here more, and, daughter, Jesus loves you. Seek Him during and after the storms."

I wake to the ringing of my smart phone alarm. I had set it for three hours because I didn't want to sleep through the night and not go to the Jazzy Blues. When I turn to toss the quilt back, I see Mama sleeping next me.

She doesn't look like my grandma. Papa said we look like his mama, especially me. I move closer and share the pillow with her.

Her eyebrows are thin—mine are thick—and
her eyelashes are sparse. A person could sweep
with mine. Every night she rolls and ties her hair
no matter how tired or drunk she is. Most nights
mine is all over my head, but luckily she just
pressed it, so it won't be that tangled. I'm not
tender-headed anyway, but she is. I remember
her eyes watering under Grandma's comb.

She blows a long breath, moans, and blinks
open her eyes. "Hey."

"Hey," I answer.

"You dreamed about her didn't you?"

"Yeah, we were all in the church."

"Who do you think the 'he' is?"

"I think it's Uncle Doug."

"Me too."

"Is he going to die or move out?"

"I think it's more serious than him moving
out."

"Are you going to say anything to him?"

"What can I say? I am going to take her advice
and enjoy every day with him that I can."

"It seems like we should tell him something, a
warning, or something?"

"What would you warn him against? Walking
outside, driving? No, it's best for him if we say
nothing."

"Did you see her earlier, at the church?"

"You know I did. I have felt her all along, just like you, and now she is gone."

"With Papa."

"I hope so. What happens after people die is a mystery to me."

"Are you going to start going to church?"

"We will see. And your Uncle Doug was right. Nelson is too old for you. And he was right about you. You got a lot more going for you than dating older men. You can stand on your own ten toes, and I can't wait to see you do it, baby. No dating Nelson Brown for you, understand? Your grandmother wouldn't like it."

And I do. My mama thinks I can make it in the world without doing what she did. I like that, a lot. "Yes, Mama, I do understand." And understanding has me feeling a little grown and special to her.

When I call Edith to tell her we are not going, I can hear in her voice that she has been crying. I put the phone on speaker because my toenail is caught on my grandma's quilt, and I need my hands to free it without tearing my toenail or the quilt.

"Oh, that's okay, May. I don't think I could have made it anyway."

I am tired, but something is wrong with Edith, so I ask, "You want to come over? Maybe watch some TV, and have a sleepover downstairs like we used to?"

I can hear the sadness all in her voice. "I should come over. You know, Mooky was living here with my mama, him and Blake. She smokes crack with them. She smokes crack all day and all night, but I still try to look out for her because sometimes she's just not right in the head. That stuff messes with her thinking."

"Dang." I didn't mean to say that out loud. I think she needs a little bit more from me than "dang." "Come on over, Edith. Spend the night."

"I will be there in a couple of minutes."

When I look to the door, my mama is standing there looking at me. "You don't know do you?"

"Mmph?"

"About Mooky and Edith?"

"Know what, Mama?"

"He raped her?"

No. I would have known that. I free my toenail and look at my mama. How would she know something like that happened to my friend and I didn't? "What?" I ask.

"Last summer, your uncle Doug and I drove by her wandering naked in the street. She was so confused. She fought him, but Doug got her in the car, and we drove her to the hospital. She kept screaming Mooky's name and screaming for her mother. After they got her settled at the hospital, we drove back to her house.

"When I got to her mother's house to tell her what happened, she was sitting up in the front room with Mooky and Blake smoking crack. She didn't try to hide it. I told her we took Edith to the hospital because she was raped, and that woman told me Edith was putting on and wasn't nothing really wrong with her.

"I went back to the hospital, and I asked Edith did she want to move in with us. She said no. I left her a couple hundred dollars to stay in a hotel for a couple of days, but I don't know what she did."

My mama lowers her head, turns from me, and walks away.

I hear Edith and my mama in the living room. They are sitting on the couch. My mama has her arms around Edith, and they are both crying.

"She is so sick, Ms. Joyce. I pray for her all the time, but all she cares about is crack. Pastor came over and laid hands on her, but two days later she was back to smoking that stuff. I have to keep my money on me because she will take any- and everything I have, and she lets anybody in our house. Anybody. I'm scared for her. That's way I don't leave, but I can't stay much longer.

It's her or me, and I don't want to sacrifice myself for her. I don't."

Edith cries some more, and I walk back to my bedroom. Edith spent the night but with Mama, not me.

Chapter Seventeen

Early Sunday morning, standing at the kitchen sink picking greens, I don't feel all that special. Really, the special feeling left after I mopped the bathroom floors, and took out the garbage. I saw Carlos walking back from the store with a dozen eggs. Instead of going home with the eggs, he brought them over to my house to cook while we talked.

He loves sunny-side up runny fried eggs and toast. He likes to sop up the yoke with toast, and that is what he is doing while I am picking the greens.

"So what did Walter's mama say?" I ask.

"She said the lawyer wanted five grand, but he couldn't promise anything more than a public defender, so she is going with a public defender. She said the whole robbery attempt is on tape, and that Walter is screwed. Those were her exact words: 'Walter is screwed.'"

"Dang, are you going to see him?"

"I'ma try to go tomorrow after school."

"Cool, I will go with you."

"We talked to the Ohio State people."

"And?"

"My mama said everything is settled. Nothing was affected. I will be balling at Ohio State this fall."

"You go, boy!" I scream, and I am truly happy for him. I must be because I start crying when I am happy, and I feel the tears.

"Why are you crying?"

"Because I love you, stupid. And I want things to work out for you, and it looks like they are."

I see all his teeth because of his big smile.

On Monday after school, my mama will not let me go visit Walter. She says visiting men in jail shouldn't be part of my life experience.

"An acceptance of men who go to jail will lower your standards in men. If you start visiting jailbirds now, you will be visiting them for the rest of your life. You don't want the negative jail atmosphere in your psyche."

I thought she was kidding, but I have been standing in her bedroom begging her for thirty minutes. I now see that she is serious, but I'm not really that upset about not going see Walter. I just didn't want to leave Carlos hanging.

Walter is nice and all, but him being gone is not a problem. He was starting to be a real pest. Besides, I used his getting locked up in a lie. I told Samuel he was my high school boyfriend, and that he didn't have to worry about me dating him anymore. That pleased Samuel.

I leave Mama in her room painting her toenails, and I walk to the kitchen to tell Carlos he's going to have to go by himself. In the kitchen, Carlos is sitting at the table on his phone.

"Are you sure? Okay, thanks for the information." He clicks off and looks up at me and says, "You have to be twenty-one to visit or be with an adult, and you have to be on a list. Just his mama and the lawyer are on his list right now. We can't go."

I sit at the table with him. "Mama wasn't going to let me go anyway. She says visiting people in jail will affect my character."

"What?"

"Nothing. I can't go."

"I need to get home. See ya later." He hoists his book bag from the floor to his shoulder and exits without buttoning up his coat and with his hat in his hand. For some reason, my mind goes to Mooky while watching the door close. *Dang, he's dead. And Walter is in jail.*

I go to take a shower before work, and I get a little sick. I am throwing up when my mama comes bursting into the bathroom. She tells me, "Pregnancy is contagious. It spreads faster than the flu," and she slams the door without saying another word.

That kind of freaks me out, and it makes me think about my pills. I haven't taken one in a couple of days. I peep out of the bathroom door before I exit. My mama really spooked me. In my room, I pull the pills free. I haven't taken one in four days, dang. So, I take three.

Edith is outside waiting so we can walk to work together. She still hasn't told me about Mooky raping her, and I haven't asked.

"Hey, girl, how was school?" I ask pulling my phone out to call Samuel.

"School was cool, but your mama and the guidance counselor are adding confusion to a simple situation. I was going to graduate and go to work, but both them are trying to convince me to go to college and become an RN as opposed to a CNA. But neither of them have to live with my mother.

Today, the counselor gave me some options about living on campus right here in the city. It seems having good grades gives me choices."

I stop walking and dialing Samuel's number, and I just look at my friend. "Wow, you just said a mouthful. Good grades got you choices. I need to get my butt in to see my guidance counselor and see my choices too."

Calling Samuel doesn't seem that important. I put the phone back into my pocket. When we talk on the phone now, he begs for sex more than Walter ever did.

The phone is vibrating in my coat pocket. Of course, it is a text from Samuel. He is asking me to ditch school tomorrow. I ignore it. No way I'm ditching school. I have to get in to see my guidance counselor. He sends another text.

I love you.

I don't love him. He's cool and fine, but I am thinking that there are way more cool and fine dudes out there for me to meet. Being in love is an end to all, and I am not ready to end anything. I am just getting started.

I ignore his text and go to work.

All during work, he keeps calling and texting. From his texts, I understand that he wants to bring us dinner: Mama, Uncle Doug, and me. That way he can get to see me. I think it's a cool idea, sort of, and Mama agrees, so I dial Samuel's number, and he answers on the second ring.

"Hey, how is my woman doing?"

Him calling me his woman doesn't excite me like it used to.

"I'm good, but my mama said don't get here after eight. She said if you can't make it before then don't come." She didn't say that, but I am hoping he can't make it because I have a lot of homework.

"That's cool. I'm ten minutes away with the steaks."

"Okay, see you in a minute."

I drop down on the couch. Uncle Doug is walking out the front door.

"Going to get your mama some lotto tickets and wine. You want something?" he asks zipping up his big green coat.

"No, I am good, but dinner is on its way."

A smirk comes to his face. "I know." He pulls the front door closed behind himself.

The steaks, salad, and soup are on the dining room table, but Mama has Samuel and me

sitting on the couch in the living room waiting
for Uncle Doug. She's sitting on the window
ledge telling Samuel about Uncle Doug.

"He is a butcher. He learned how to cut meat
down South, and he's been doing it up here for
years. Once he gets his license, we will get married. We're setting the date, so one celebration
will do for both. You like my ring?" My mama
holds up her hand for Samuel's appraisal.

"Oh, yes, now that is a rock."

Mama laughs. "He surprised me with it.
Proposed right there in the jewelry store."

If I didn't know my mama, I would think she
was getting a little weepy. She stands and says,
"He's here." Mama holds the front door open for
Uncle Doug.

"Brr, it's colder than a well digger's prick out
there, and some fool now parked in my spot.
You think after I shot the windows out of that
last fool's car no other fool would park there. Go
get my shotgun, Gloria. These boys around here
don't think fat meat is greasy. I ain't playin' wid
'em."

Samuel stands. "Sir, I may have mistakenly
parked in your spot. I parked in front of the
house."

"Why would you do that, boy? Take another
man's spot?"

"I wasn't thinking, sir, but I will move my car."

"You cain't. I now already slashed yo' tire. Damn, boy, you ain't that bright, is you? Parking in another man's spot. May, if this is the boy bringing our supper you better check the food fo' freshness. Seems like I smell some bad meat in here."

"Oh, no, sir, those steaks are fresh."

"Naw, I smell old meat, and I knows old meat." He hands Mama her lotto tickets and wine, and he unzips his coat. "Let me go over and look at that meat."

We all follow him into the dining room.

"Aw naw, boy, this meat is bad. Y'all don't smell that? We ain't eating that rotten crap."

Uncle Doug picks the steaks up with his hand and walks through the kitchen door with them. We hear him step on the garbage can pedal, raising the lid, and we hear the steaks hitting the plastic bag.

"That boy tryin' to give us all food poisonin'."

Samuel's mouth drops open, and his hand goes to his forehead. "Those streaks were fresh," he tells Mama and me.

We all look to the kitchen door as it swings open, and Uncle Doug comes through grinning from ear to ear with the steaks on a platter and a bottle of steak sauce in his hand.

"Let's eat."

I think Samuel might have peed his pants.

"My tires?"

"The car is fine, boy. Let's eat."

Chapter Eighteen

I can't go to sleep because things are weird in my head right now. I have fluffed the pillows, pulled the cover sheet up and down, thrown Grandma's quilt back and pulled it back up ten times. The green letters on the clock read TUESDAY, 3:15. I have to be up for school at 6:15. Having Samuel over for dinner put weird things in my mind, and Uncle Doug living here is not helping the weirdness.

Mama said the less Uncle Doug sees of Samuel, the better. She said he won't stop fussing with her about me not dating boys my own age, and he went so far as suggesting that I go to church with him where he would introduce me to some nice young Christian boys. Mama said we are going to church with him on his birthday next Sunday. That's all he wants for a birthday present: us going to his church and meeting his pastor. Weird.

Mama closed the store for good because Uncle Doug told her he would take care of all the house bills and my allowance. He said, "It's too dangerous nowadays to have strangers comin' to the door all times of mornin' on the weekends. Mooky and 'em ain't the only desperate crackheads in the neighborhood."

I didn't mind closing the store. I thought Mama would, but she didn't. She did not say one word in protest, just, "Okay, Doug." And she's been saying that a lot, "Okay, Doug," and it's been weird.

What else is weird is no Carlos or Walter. Carlos is always working, so I don't see too much of him. And all of school feels weird, like I should have been finished a long time ago. I can't wait to graduate. Nappy-headed Ms. Stockton found me a theater school in New York City, and I'm really thinking about going. The brochures look nice, and Mama promises that the money for school is there. Theater school. That won't be weird.

I sleep a little, and then I get up for the bathroom. I feel like I am going to be sick again, but nothing happens. I go to the kitchen and pack my book bag, cook my oatmeal, check the e-mails on my phone, and then stand in the door with my coat on waiting for the bus.

Uncle Doug walks into the living room in his sweatpants and thermal T-shirt. "Yo' school is closed. All the schools is closed because it is twenty below zero outside."

"Twenty below?"

"Yep, they closed the schools. Your mama and me going up to the Michigan City outlet mall. You welcome to ride with us."

"I could have still been asleep." I let my book bag fall from my shoulder to the floor. I didn't get two hours' worth of sleep last night. I want to curse, but instead, I peel off my beige wool coat and hang it back in the closet and do an about-face and head for my bed.

"We leaving here about eight," Uncle Doug says to my back.

I don't remove my clothes to get under the covers. I fluff the pillow and let my head drop.

"Oh, no, you don't," comes from my bedroom doorway. "Since you up, come help me load this store stock into Doug's trunk. He's got a cousin in Gary who is going to buy it all from us."

"Mama, I can't. I didn't sleep at all last night."

"I know, I heard you tossing and turning. But you dressed, so come on and help me do this. Then I will let you go back to sleep. Get up, get up, get up!"

She is not going to stop until I get up, so I throw the covers back and get up.

She didn't let me go back to sleep, not even on the ride to Michigan City. She and Uncle Doug have pulled me into their honeymoon plans like it all is going to happen next week. They came out here to the outlet to shop for honeymoon clothes.

We are shopping for Mama's swimsuits now, and the problem is she looks good in all of them, and she can't pick just one. I think she wants Uncle Doug to pick one out, but I don't think he cares. Uncle Doug has a bag of fresh shrimp in the car, and he wants to go home and make a pot of gumbo. We have been talking about it all day. He got the crab meat, the okra, and sausages from his cousin in Gary who bought the store stock.

"Get the pink, the yellow, and the green one," he says to the dressing room curtain. He just messed up because there is no green one. He is sitting by the curtain in a chair, and he has it rocked back on its legs.

"What green one?" Mama asks.

"The one that tied at the chest."

"That's blue, fool."

Dang, he is paying attention.

"Whatever color it is, get them three and let's go."

"Are you rushing me, Douglas?"

"Yes, I am. This girl is hungry, and me and her been waitin' all day to get to those shrimps."

"I ain't heard a complaint from the girl. All I hear is your mouth."

"That's 'cause she out here gnawin' on her lips she so hungry."

"Oh, you need to stop lying on my child like that."

Mama pulls the curtain back and emerges dressed. In her arms are the three swimsuits Uncle Doug suggested. "Let's go. I want some gumbo too."

Grandma's big stainless-steel pot is simmering and filled almost to the brim. The whole house smells like Uncle Doug's gumbo. The scent of stewing crab legs and shrimp, sausage and chicken, rice and okra, and gumbo filé spice boiling pulled me out of my room and to the kitchen table. Uncle Doug has set the table with three bowls, and each has a tablespoon in it. A big ol' tablespoon. What was he thinking? I don't say anything critical because he is so happy with himself.

"You gonna like this. Give it about ten more minutes then we gonna throw down."

"Throw down?" I ask.

"Wait, what do y'all say? Um, 'we gonna get our eat on.'"

"I hear you, Uncle Doug."

Mama comes into the kitchen with her gun cleaning kit and two pistols in her arms. Uncle Doug looks up from his pot and says, "I know you ain't gonna clean those pistols in here while I'm cookin'."

"Why not? I clean my guns in here all the time." When she gets to the table, she stumbles slightly, and everything in her grasp hits the table.

The black case that holds the kit stuff lands on one of its corners and bounces toward me. I catch it. The .22 revolver lands flat on its side and spins a little. The .45 automatic lands on the butt and releases a round.

The shot is so loud that I hunch my shoulders and dive from the chair to the floor. I look up to Mama, and her eyes are blinking nonstop. She is shook. I look over to Uncle Doug at the stove, and his shoulders are hunched, and his head is at a strange angle, and something has gotten into his thin black hair. He must have dropped his mixing spoon in the gumbo and splashed some of it up in his hair.

No.

It's not gumbo.

Oh, God.

It's blood.

Uncle Doug drops to his knees then over to his left. The mixing spoon falls from his right hand.

Mama screams and runs over to him. I go to the stove and push Grandma's stainless-steel pot to the back burner and cut the gas off. When I look down, I see blood coming out of two spots in Uncle Doug's head.

The ambulance people take him out of the kitchen on a stretcher. When Uncle Doug gets outside, they put him on a gurney and pull a sheet over his head. Mama won't move away from the gurney. It takes three police officers to pull her away from Uncle Doug, but then she falls in the grass and balls up in a knot. No matter what I say, she won't unwind. Ms. Carol and me try to get her up, but we can't.

The ambulance lady says my mama is in shock. They put her on a stretcher and load her in the ambulance with Uncle Doug. I try to climb in too, but Ms. Carol wraps her arms around me and pulls me away.

"I'ma take you up there, baby. I'ma take you. Come on with me, May."

When Carlos and I walk in to the packed emergency room, we stand by the doors. We are not sure of where to go or who to talk to. Ms. Carol comes through automatic doors and walks straight up to the guard at the desk.

"I'm here to see about my sister, Gloria Joyce. The ambulance just brought her here."

The guard taps the keyboard in front of him. "She's in ER." He hands her two white sticky visitor passes. "Through these doors and see the nurse at the desk." He buzzes open the half-wood and half-chrome doors behind him. Ms. Carol grabs my hand, and we walk through the doors.

I see Mama right away. She is still in a knot on the gurney. I go to her, and Ms. Carol goes to the nurse behind a tall desk.

"Mama. Mama, can you hear me? Can you hear me, Mama?" I reach for her fisted hand. I cover her fist with both my hands. "Mama." I bend down to get closer to her ear. "Mama."

"She will be all right in about twenty minutes," a voice from behind me says. "The sedative will start working soon."

I look up to see the ambulance lady who was at our house. "Can she hear me?"

"No, darling, she can't. Not yet. Give her about twenty more minutes."

"Can I sit here with her?"

"Yes, you can. Your aunt is taking care of the paperwork. God bless, baby." And the ambulance lady walks away.

I need my grandmother, Papa, Mama, some-body.

***

It's been three hours, and Mama is still in a knot. There are two doctors and a nurse over here with us. The nurse gives her a shot, and Mama's fingers spread open, her eyes open, and she looks right at me. I move to her, but she starts jerking all over. The doctor pushes me away from her, and the nurse draws a curtain. I try to move past the curtain, but the other doctor comes out, and we bump into each other.

To Ms. Carol, a doctor says, "We are going to ask you folks to go back outside into the waiting area. The nurse will notify you when the procedure is done."

"Why can't we stay?" I ask.

"The procedure is difficult for family to witness, trust us. The nurse will be out to you shortly."

I hear my mama jumping around behind that curtain. "That nurse gave her the wrong stuff," I yell into his face.

"No, her reaction was expected, just not so soon. Please go into the waiting area."

I'm not leaving, but Ms. Carol grabs my hand and pulls me away from the doctor and through the two chrome and wood doors.

The waiting room is less crowded, and Carlos calls us over to two seats under the television. "How's your mama? She's okay, right?"

"No, she's not okay. They are doing something to her that we can't watch. I saw her look at me, but then she . . ." I'm starting to cry. All this is too much. "She's not okay," I say and get up and walk out the automatic doors to go outside.

I take the sidewalk all the way to the street. I'm glad they didn't try to follow me. My mama better be all right. If they hurt my mama in there, me and Uncle Doug will get them.

Oh, shit. Oh, shit. Oh, shit. Uncle Doug, no, no, no, not Uncle Doug. They are going to take my mama to jail. It was an accident. I saw it. That nurse gave my mama the wrong stuff. *Not Uncle Doug, and not my mama.*

"Dang, dang, dang." I dial Samuel's number.

"Hey, baby," he answers, and I am relieved. His voice mail would have put me over the edge. I needed to talk to him.

"My mama, my mama, she shot Uncle Doug by mistake. He died, and she is in the hospital."

"What hospital, babe?"

"At the university," is all I can say. I drop my arm and collapse to the street curb. I sit, and I cry.

They are going to take my mama to jail. I try to stand to go back into the ER, but I can't. I stumble like a drunk person. My legs are too weak, so I sit some more and cry some more. I am getting cold, so I try again and, as soon as I am up, Samuel and his little red car pull up.

"Here I am," he says like I can't see the car right in front of me.

I walk to the passenger side and get in. I hope he doesn't ask me what happened because that will start the tears again. I close the car door. He leans over and kisses me on the cheek. The heat in the car feels good.

"I know a place where you can get something to eat, and I can get a drink. Okay?"

"I can't go far."

"The place is three blocks away. Buckle up."

He orders me a cheeseburger that I can't eat, but he drinks his drink. We are standing at a bar, a smoke-filled bar that reeks, but I do feel better being with him. I told him about my mama and Uncle Doug on the drive over.

"It sounds like your mother is in shock, May. She will get better. And, don't worry, the police will deduce that it was an accident. Everything will be fine, babe."

I lean to him and kiss him on the cheek. "I hope so." But I am worried. I tell him, "They are going to put my mama in jail."

"No, they will understand it was an accident."

"I don't know."

"I know. Relax. Let's get back to the hospital. Are you ready to leave?" He places his little glass on the bar top.

I see her in the mirror walking up behind us before she speaks: "And where are you taking this child?"

I have seen her in pictures on his phone and in his wallet. This is Samuel's wife standing behind us.

"I asked you a question, Sam. What are you doing here with this child?"

I need to leave, right now. I can walk the three blocks to the hospital. When I look at Samuel's reflection in the mirror, I am confused. His face is smiling, and he looks happy.

"Hey, baby!" he says standing and turning around. He pulls her into an embrace. "I didn't think my text went through. So, you are good with going out to eat tonight?"

"What text? I saw your Porsche outside and couldn't figure out why you would be in a dive like this."

Still hugging her, he says, "Oh, me and May stopped to go over her lines. She is an understudy in the Langston play, and she's trying out for a role at Loyola. I was going to drop her off then meet you at Geno's for steaks. That is, if you're up for it."

He is still hugging her.

"Of course, baby, I would love to stop for steaks." She kisses him, breaks the embrace, and turns to me and says, "It's nice meeting you, May. I hope you get the part." She extends her hand for me to shake.

I don't know what to say, but I smile my biggest smile and shake her hand.

"I can walk from here. You don't need to drop me off," I say to Samuel, but his wife is still holding my hand, so I can't leave. She is starting to squeeze my hand. And when I look at her she is no longer smiling.

"Oh, my God, what are you doing?" Samuel screams.

I look down and see blood.

She spins me around and puts a bloody razor to my neck.

Samuel pulls a gun from underneath his jacket. I never knew he carried a gun.

He tells his wife, "Drop it."

She says, "Fuck you and this little slut. I know you have been screwing her at your brother's house. I'm going to kill the ho!"

And that's when I see the fire leap out of his gun.

Chapter Nineteen

Oh, I was asleep. It was all a dream. When I open my eyes, I will be in my room, and everything will be how it was before the dream. When I open my eyes, everything will be just fine. I know it.

I open my eyes, and everything is not fine. I am in a hospital room. I reach for the cup of ice water, and I sip from the straw. My mind is so mixed up. I put the cup down and settle back into the pillow.

I was shaking his wife's hand. She was smiling and holding my hand too tight, way too tight. But, all I felt was her squeezing my hand. I didn't feel anything else, but I remember now. I didn't feel her cutting me, but I saw the blood after Samuel screamed, "Oh, my God! What are you doing?"

She was cutting me while she was shaking my hand and smiling, and I didn't feel it. I sit up and pull the sheets back to see the damage. There are three rows of stiches on my left thigh and four on my right. They are covered with some type of clear-looking tape that looks like a wrap more than a bandage. His wife was smiling and squeezing my hand while she was slicing my thighs with a straight razor.

When Samuel first showed me a picture of her on the bus, I remember thinking she looked crazy. I tried to pull away from her after I discovered that she was cutting me, but she had a tight grip on my hand. She spun me around so that she was behind me, and she put the straight razor to my neck. That's when Samuel pointed his gun at us.

He told his wife, "Drop it."

She said, "Fuck you and this little slut."

And that's when I saw the fire leap out of his gun. I am tired of remembering. I close my eyes.

"May, can you hear me, baby?"

I hear her, but my eyes won't open and neither will my mouth. But I hear her.

"Squeeze my hand, baby. If you can hear me, squeeze my hand."

I hear, but I don't feel her hand or mine.

"When will she snap out of it, Doctor?"

"I'm not a doctor. I'm a nurse, and that is a question I can't answer. We weren't expecting this. She was progressing. She came out of surgery strong and alert. She asked for water and a sponge bath to cool down."

"Where is the doctor?"

"She has two, and they both want to speak with you."

It's my mama. I hear her. It's my mama.

"She has been in a coma for sixteen hours that we know of."

"She sleeps pretty hard. Are you sure she's not sleeping?"

"No, Ms. Joyce, this isn't sleep. Her brainwave patterns are not consistent with sleep."

"When will she be better?"

"That is hard to say. We didn't see this coming. The wounds on her thighs are seriously infected. We have put her on stronger antibiotics, and the nurses have orders to flush the wounds every three hours. A specialist has been called to help with the infection. She will see her tonight, and I will have more information for you after her visit."

"Is her life in danger, Doctor?"

"Not if we can treat the infection and stop it from spreading. I believe once we have eliminated that from her body things will take a turn for the better. The blade she was cut with had to be bacteria-ridden. If we could find the knife that would improve our chances."

"I don't know who cut or shot her. I was told she died. I came here expecting to identify my baby's body, but she is alive. Alive, Doctor, and now you are telling me she is in a coma. Believe it or not, that is good news. Damn good news."

I hear them, clearly. But, I don't feel myself breathing or feel any part on my body. I am all thoughts and their words. Samuel's wife cut me with an infected straight razor. She must hate me, a lot.

I can't stay here, wherever here is. I have things to do, and I need to see my mama. She wasn't doing well. The last thing she needs is to be worrying about me. I love my mama. I loved Uncle Doug, too. I got to go, to wake up or something.

"Doctor!"

I hear her my mama yelling.

I got to leave this place of nothingness.

"Doctor!"

I feel her touching my shoulder.

"Doctor!"

My eyes are open, and I see the light she is shining into my right eye.

"Can you follow it?"

"Yes."

"Well, please do it," she asks.

I didn't know she wanted me to follow the light. She only asked if I could. I follow the silly light. "I'm very hungry," I tell the doctor and the nurse.

"That's good," the doctor answers.

"I'll order you something right away," the nurse says.

"Was my mother here?"

"Yes, and I will call her, too," the nurse says.

"You responded well to the antibiotics and the blood transfusion from your brother. You had quite an infection, young lady. The most severe I have seen in several years. You are extremely healthy with a very strong immune system." The doctor places her hand on my shoulder. "I have never seen a patient so infected respond so quickly. I am keeping you on the drip and will check on you later tonight and in the morning. I am sure your regular doctor will stop by as well." She clicks off the little light, shakes her head, and smiles. "You are a miracle."

Dang, how sick was I? And what brother? "I am very tired and hungry."

"Two very good signs."

"Hey."

I open my eyes and see my mama.

"Did you know that you are pregnant?" Her eyebrows rise.

"What?"

"You pregnant, baby."

"No, it's a mistake. I miss my period all the time."

"May, they had to give you blood to save the baby. You are pregnant."

If I am pregnant, why is she smiling?

"And guess whose blood they had to use?"

"Mama, I am not pregnant." When I try to sit up my arm, shoulder, and my thighs hurt bad enough to stop me from moving.

"You had a horrible infection, and you survived because of your brother."

"Mama, you must be really sick. I need to talk to somebody else. I need to know what happened to me." I don't have a brother. My mama is going through something. I need to talk to someone else. Uncle Doug's death is messing with her mind.

"Ain't nobody going to tell you any different than what I am telling you. Your brother saved your life."

"Mama, what brother? What are you talking about?"

She blows a breath and sits back in the chair. "I wasn't ever going to tell you, but after Doug, and after you almost died, and after talking to Carol, and we been talking a lot lately, things are just different. You never know when your time is up, baby. Death just comes. We, Carol and me, decided it wasn't right that y'all didn't know. Life is too short for secrets."

I don't know what she's talking about, but the pain is spreading up my arm and down my back and now my thighs are starting to hurt more. "Mama, would you call a nurse? The pain is getting worse."

She doesn't hesitate to leave my bedside and the room.

Pregnant? Nope, can't be. That man is married.

The door opens, but it's not the nurse. It's Carlos. "Hey there, sis. And I mean that fo' real." He bends down and kisses me on the cheek and keeps talking.

"Your heart stopped, and the doctors still haven't figured out why. You got shot in the shoulder, but your heart stopped, and that's why they said you were dead. Your body just shut down. It's real good to see that you're all right. You scared me, girl, real bad. And since you been out, nothing but strange stuff has been happening."

He sits in the chair Mama left empty.

"First, think about this, you being my natural sister. And our mamas would have kept it a secret if Uncle Doug hadn't died. They have been holding this secret all our lives. We have the same daddy."

He says it like he's talking about candy or something: I got some Sugar Babies and you got some Sugar Babies. What the hell is he talking about? I need the nurse.

"And you know what else was a trip? Your mama. Once she heard you got hurt, she snapped to and broke out of whatever spell had her. And I'ma tell you something else that is strange, her and my mama been together like we be talking. Lately, you don't see one without the other."

I hear him, but he's fading away.

When I wake up, Carlos is gone. A nurse is at my bedside, and Ms. Carol is in the chair on the side of the bed.

"The doctor won't order a stronger painkiller because of the baby. The medicine in the IV will keep you sleeping. We will fight the pain like that for a while, understand?" the nurse says.

I just nod my head because my throat feels sore.

"Good. You are doing well. Such a strong girl. And that baby is strong, too." She lays my wrist back down and fluffs my pillow.

"I have the night shift," Ms. Carol says as the nurse turns and leaves. "Your mama wants to be here when the doctors are here, so she has the day shift, and Carlos and Edith have been here the afternoons. How are you feeling?"

"I don't know. I think I am okay, but I don't know when I am awake or asleep. Are Carlos and I brother and sister?"

"Yes."

"Did my mama shoot Uncle Doug in the head?"

"Yes."

"And?"

"Yes, baby, he's dead."

"And my friend Samuel, he shot me?"

"Yes."

"And did his wife cut me?"

"Yes, baby, she did. She's crazy. And that Samuel character got arrested, too, but the people in the bar came to his aid and told the police he was trying to save you."

"Then I must really be pregnant?"

"Yes, you are."

"Mmm," is all I can manage. I am having Samuel Talbert's baby. "He's married," I say out loud, but I meant to think it.

"I know. Your mama told me. She wanted to call him, but I told her to wait and let you talk to him first."

"I don't know what to say," I tell her. "I never told anyone I was carrying their child."

"The call is about intentions. The call is to find out what he plans to do."

"I should just get rid of it."

"Really?"

"No, I couldn't."

"Once you get out of this hospital, we will have plenty of time to think things through."

"Oh, my God, I just thought about something. I will be walking across the graduation stage fat with a baby. Oh, no, I can't do that. I just can't."

"Why not? I walked across the stage with Carlos sitting in the audience. I did it because it was my diploma. I earned it, and I earned it while being a teenager with a baby. Getting pregnant as a kid wasn't smart, but I was determined to graduate on time. I was determined to finish because everybody, and I mean everybody, said I wouldn't. But I did, and I did it with a child.

"The baby is here, May. You are pregnant, and life goes on. So put your big girl panties on and deal with it, but don't forget you have help, baby. Me and your mama are here for you."

I don't even try to fight the sleep because all of this—the baby, the pain, Ms. Carol and Mama, me and Carlos, and Uncle Doug—it is all too much.

***

I smell his Gucci cologne. I feel his lips kissing my check, and I hear him saying, "I love you, baby."

I open my eyes to Samuel Talbert and decide not to play around with it. "I'm pregnant with your baby."

"Our baby," he says. "And I know. Your Mama came to see me at work this morning. I bet it's a girl, and she is going to be as beautiful as you."

Has the whole world gone mad? "You are married. What are you talking about?"

"So, I was married when you met me, and now you are pregnant with my baby. Nothing much changes. I will do for you as I have always done, and when the baby gets here I will do for her, and she will have my name. None of this involves my wife. Our thing is our thing. I can take care of you and my daughter. You know this."

"What are you saying?"

"I'm saying relax. I got this. My name goes on the birth certificate. Nothing changes except we have a baby now."

"So, wait. What you are saying is that you stay married, and I stay your chick on the side only with a baby?"

"Yeah, nothing changes but the baby."

"So what will the baby call you, Uncle Samuel?"

"My daughter will call me Daddy. What's with you, May? Never mind, I know you have been through a lot. Don't worry, baby, I got you and our daughter."

"What about your crazy wife? Do you have her too?"

"Yeah, she has some issues. She is in a private psych ward in Dallas. Her father flew her out right after the police released her. Her lawyer says you need to sign papers not to press charges. Okay?"

"She tried to kill me, Samuel, and you shot me! I need you to leave, right now. Nurse! Nurse!"

He hurries out with my second scream.

He's got me. Yeah, as long as I don't say a thing about his crazy wife and stay a secret, me and my baby stay a secret.

All of this is bullshit: walking across the graduation stage fat with a baby and being Samuel Talbert's outside family. Neither one of these thoughts is comfortable for me. I am not walking across that stage big with pregnancy. They will just have to mail me the diploma or something.

The outside family situation is bigger than my brain right now. I don't love Samuel enough to think about me and him being married with a family, but I never thought about being anybody's outside family, nor have I really thought about being the other woman or the other family.

I guess I am his other woman, and when the baby comes, we will be his other family. Hell no. I don't like the sound or feel of that. "Other" in front of the word "woman" feels less than, and it's worse in front of the word "family." No, I am not going to be anybody's other anything. No, it's not worth it. I am not about to spend my life being his other family. I have things to do with my life. He's got me. I don't want him to have me. I've got me and, if I am pregnant, I've got my baby, too.

I do not want to be with Samuel or bothered by his crazy wife.

Now, that thought feels good in my head.

I wake to hearing my mama humming one of Grandma's favorite songs, "When the Saints Go Marching In." When she sees I am awake, she stops. "Hey, baby. I talked to Samuel this morning."

"Yeah, he stopped by."

"I know. He told me he was going to put his name on the birth certificate when the baby comes. Didn't that make you happy? And he wrote me a check for three thousand dollars to help with things. He said he understands that things are going to be difficult with Doug gone. I like that young man."

"Mama, please give him that check back."

"What? Why?"

"I am finished with Samuel."

"Finished? Girl, you are having his child. What kind of foolishness has gotten into you today? Oh, it must be the medicine. You are not thinking right."

"No, Mama, I am thinking right."

"Did you hear me? The check was for three thousand dollars, and he wrote it like he was writing a thirty dollar check. Child, you got pregnant by the right one. That boy has money."

"Mama, I don't want him or his money."

"You may not want it, but you do need it. No, we need it. You got a baby coming, and it's just you and me, so we ain't turning down nothing. Give the check back? Shit, I now already cashed the check and spent most of it. And it will never be over with you and Samuel. You got a baby by his rich ass."

I lift my head from the pillow as much as I can and look right into her face and say, "You had a baby by my father, and I don't even know his name. So don't tell me it can't be over because I am pregnant."

If I weren't in a hospital bed, that statement would have gotten me slapped, and I know it.

She blinks her eyes a couple of times and blows a long breath and says, "That was different. All your daddy had was charm and a damn good singing voice. He sang me out of my drawers. I was young and stupid and believed his lies. He told the same lies to Carol. You and Carlos were born two days apart. He probably fucked Carol and me on the same day. Eric Milk is your daddy's name. The last I heard, he was living on the streets in Detroit. I didn't and don't care a rat's ass about him. He broke my heart with Carol. After I found about her, I never said his name again to anyone."

Still looking in her face, I say, "So, if he would have had money, it would have been different? Him breaking your heart would have been acceptable if he had money?"

"No, that man cut me to the bone. It was over."

"It's over with me and Samuel."

"But, you don't understand what you are walking away from. You don't understand how much easier your life will be with this man in it. I can't let you do that, May."

"Mama, I can take care of myself. We can take care of ourselves. I don't want to owe Samuel anything."

"But, he already owes you, baby. That's what you don't understand. That man planted his seed in you, and he is responsible for it and you for the next eighteen years, and I am not going to let you walk away from that support. If, after the baby comes, you don't want to be with him, fine. Y'all will work that out. But, for now, we need his money. Let that man help us."

"But, Mama, I don't want to be you. I don't want to be messing with married men for their money. I don't want to be the other woman."

Nothing I say is going to change my mama's mind, and I am tired of talking. I turn away from her and face the curtain and let my eyes close.

I see my grandmother's face. She is smiling at me. She was no one's other woman. Grandma was Papa's wife. Mama is acting like she has forgotten that she came from a family, not an outside family. I came from a family. My baby will come from a family, my family, not Samuel's outside family.

When I wake, my mama is still here. "What, you thought it was over? Little girl, let me tell you something: my being the 'other woman' clothed and fed you for seventeen years. It bought you dancing lessons and acting lessons, and braces for your buckteeth and knock-knee. Understand this, child: your grandparents helped, but it was and is I who provide for your spoiled ass.

"It was me, myself, and I who paid the rent for you to live in their house, and bought the food you ate while in their house. All those damn Barbie dolls, cars, and houses came from my 'other woman' ass. All those Jordans, jeans, and jewelry I bought. Summer camps, modeling camps, Judo, Rollerblades, computer, iPhone all came from me. So, Miss Ann, if you can be half the bitch I have been to you, that seed growing inside of your selfish ass might just stand a chance.

"And understand this: I pay to extend the health insurance from your granddaddy's plan that covers your being up in this hospital. You don't want to be me. That is some funny shit. Oh, and check this out, Ms. May Diane Joyce, the doctors say you are being discharged tomorrow. Find a ride home."

And she gets up and leaves.

Chapter Twenty

Carlos can't miss school. I can't reach Ms. Carol. Mama won't answer her phone, so that only leaves Samuel, and he picks me up in one of those short white school buses for the disabled kids because it has a handicap lift on the side.

A nurse who I have never seen before is wheeling me through the hospital's glass doors to Samuel's short school bus. He is lowering the lift so I can be rolled in. If I could walk, I would run away from all of this: Samuel, Mama, and the baby. But I can't walk.

The nurse rolls me to Samuel and hands him a folder with my prescriptions and my outpatient appointment slips for rehab and the doctors.

"Thank you so much," he says.

"No problem," she answers and beelines right back through the doors. It's cold out here despite the bright afternoon sun.

"Okay, here we go," he says, and he pushes me up on the lift and raises me up into the bus. Inside the bus, he locks my wheelchair in place. "How long will you be chair-bound?" he asks, standing over me.

"About another week. The doctor says next week they will take the stiches out of my thighs."

"What about the cast?" He sits in the seat across the aisle.

"Another six weeks. Then they take this flexible one off and try a brace." This is how I first met Samuel, him driving a school bus and me sitting behind him, but he doesn't look as good to me now as he did then. I bet even with me in a cast and stiches he is going to say something about us having sex before we get home. "I'm going away to school, New York University, majoring in theater."

"What?"

"Yep. Ms. Carol and my school counselor are helping me with the paperwork." They are not helping yet, but they will be, and ol', nosey, nappy-headed Ms. Stockton will be happy enough to do a dance. I can't run away now, but I can lay out my plan for later.

"Cool, I am in New York all the time. I will show you around and help you get set up. Hey, do you want to try to make it up the stairs to my brother's place? I am sure I can wrestle that chair up the stairs."

I don't even answer him. When he turns and sees the look on my face, he says, "Just checking."

Theater school in New York, now that feels right in my head. Samuel is truly stupid if he thinks I am going all the way to New York to do the same thing with him there that I am doing here. If I see him in New York, it will be in passing. And if I see him first, he won't see me. It's funny how the right thought will suddenly pop up in my head. I like that about me.

When we pull up in front of the house, Mama is at the door in her housecoat kissing her friend Peter, the married flight attendant, good-bye. Edith comes running up the block pulling a suitcase, and her backpack is on her shoulders.

Samuel is lowering me to the sidewalk, and she is waiting. When I get down to the sidewalk, she grabs the chair. "Girl, your mama hired me to take care of you while you are in the cast." She pulls me off the lift platform and whispers, "And she paid me eight hundred dollars to start tonight, so I am here for you."

"Okay by me," I tell her.

But Samuel takes the chair from her, saying, "Allow me to get her up the stairs. After that, she is all yours."

He isn't playing. After he gets me in the house, he kisses me on the cheek and hits the door, going back to work. Edith goes to put up her bags, and Mama and me are alone in the living room. The room is filled with yellow and red roses.

"So, you found a ride home, huh?"

"Yep."

"The flowers are from Samuel, his condolences for Doug, I told him I didn't know how I was going to bury him, and he sent fifteen hundred dollars to help, but it turns out Doug had a pension from down South and a life insurance policy that will bury him. His ex-wife called me and informed me that the pension is hers, but she has no problem burying him with the policy, so the body is being shipped to Birmingham, Alabama."

The flowers smell real nice, fresh, like spring, like a new beginning.

"How are you, Mama? I mean really, how are you doing?" I look up at her trying to push aside the anger of her not picking me up.

What I see is that my mama is tired, real tired. "I am a solider, baby. I am always all right." But, she sits down on the couch and cries.

"I am going to miss him so much."

My mama is not all right.

"Mama, after everything is settled, I'm going to go to school in New York. You should move there with me." This is another right idea that just popped into my mind.

"What?"

I roll the chair over to her. "You should move with me. Sell this house and move to New York. Start over, us three in New York: you, the baby, and me. Let's go do something different, Mama."

"New York was a childish dream I had years ago."

"Smart people turn dreams into plans, Mama. Doug, Grandma, and Papa wouldn't want you to stay here and live unhappily. We can plan all while the baby is growing inside of me. We don't have to stay here, Mama."

She uses the sleeve of her housecoat to wipe her tears. "You would want me to go with you?"

"Yes, Mama. I need you, the baby needs you, and you need New York. It's a big city with a million chances. Go with me."

This is a good idea. I am looking at her really hard hoping she sees I really want her to go.

"Chicago is a big city," she says.

"But, New York gives you a fresh start, a chance to make it on your own. A city that big has to have thousands of GED programs. You can get your GED then go to business school. We can start new together, Mama. There is nothing holding you here. Come with us. I need you, and the baby needs you."

I can see her thinking about it, and I've got time to keep working on her. This is going to happen, my mama in New York.

She's still crying, but she looks at me and says, "A dream into a plan. I like that, May. I like that a lot."

And I do too.

When I look to the door, I see Grandma standing in the doorway, and she is smiling. I say nothing to my mother as I watch my grandmother's image fading.

Edith has wheeled me alongside the couch in the living room. She helped me dress in some purple and pink flannel pajamas and a thick white terrycloth rob that Mama stole from some downtown hotel.

Edith, Mama, and me are watching TV. The doorbell rings and out of reflex I move toward it, but only my shoulders and head move toward the vestibule, and that tickles Edith, who gets up for the door.

"Well, look at here."

I twist my neck almost backward to see who is at the door. It's Walter walking toward me smiling from ear to ear. Some people should not show all their teeth when they smile. A toothy smile isn't becoming on everyone.

"Hey, May." He bends down to kiss me, and he places a bundle of red roses in my lap.

"Hey, Walter," I say smiling back at him.

"I heard you got shot." He comes around and kneels in front of me. "Girl, you look good even shot and in a cast."

I laugh, and so does my mama. She asks him, "How long you been home, Walter?"

"Just today. I have a court date, but the judge said I wasn't a flight risk, so they let me out. I haven't been home yet." He looks down at his watch. "I been out for one hour and fifteen minutes. When I got out, I came straight here."

He grins up at me.

And dang, his grin makes me warm all over, especially in my stomach. *Wait, six weeks pregnant, dang. Walter could be the daddy too. Wouldn't that be something?* I smile toward my mama.

"What?" she asks.

"Nothing," I say and reach for Walter's hand.

And Walter and me smile at each other like we used to.